ALLEN C
S0-BWY-573
3 1833 03194 919 0

SPECIAL MESSAGE TO READERS

This book is published under the auspices of

THE ULVERSCROFT FOUNDATION

(registered charity No. 264873 UK)

Established in 1972 to provide funds for research, diagnosis and treatment of eye diseases.

Examples of contributions made are: —

A Children's Assessment Unit at Moorfield's Hospital, London.

•

Twin operating theatres at the Western Ophthalmic Hospital, London.

•

A Chair of Ophthalmology at the Royal Australian College of Ophthalmologists.

•

The Ulverscroft Children's Eye Unit at the Great Ormond Street Hospital For Sick Children, London.

You can help further the work of the Foundation by making a donation or leaving a legacy. Every contribution, no matter how small, is received with gratitude. Please write for details to:

THE ULVERSCROFT FOUNDATION,
The Green, Bradgate Road, Anstey,
Leicester LE7 7FU, England.
Telephone: (0116) 236 4325

In Australia write to:

THE ULVERSCROFT FOUNDATION,
c/o The Royal Australian College of Ophthalmologists,
27, Commonwealth Street, Sydney,
N.S.W. 2010.

THE VICTIM DIED TWICE

Detective Sergeant Lorillard, called to investigate the murder of old skinflint Carlysle Stevens, was struck first by the fact that the murder had not taken place where everyone thought it had. Secondly, he could find neither a suspect nor a motive. Finally, he discovered Katie Stevens, the widow, to be forthright and friendly, which, while pleasant enough, did not help him solve the crime. But Lorillard did eventually make an arrest. He also made a very close friend of Katie Stevens.

Books by Hunter Liggett
in the Linford Mystery Library:

THE MURDER MAZE

HUNTER LIGGETT

THE VICTIM DIED TWICE

Complete and Unabridged

LINFORD
Leicester

First published in Great Britain in 1969 by
Robert Hale Limited
London

First Linford Edition
published 2000
by arrangement with
Robert Hale Limited
London

British Library CIP Data

Liggett, Hunter, *1916* –
The victim died twice.—Large print ed.—
Linford mystery library
1. Detective and mystery stories
2. Large type books
I. Title
823.9′14 [F]

ISBN 0–7089–5679–3

Published by
F. A. Thorpe (Publishing) Ltd.
Anstey, Leicestershire

Set by Words & Graphics Ltd.
Anstey, Leicestershire
Printed and bound in Great Britain by
T. J. International Ltd., Padstow, Cornwall

This book is printed on acid-free paper

1

The Passing of Carlysle Stevens

In the view of the widow, Carlysle Stevens deserved from Fate about what he got.

Katherine Stevens was that kind of woman. Plain, sturdy, unattractive, solidly built, eminently practical and pithily forthright.

If she had an objection it was with the manner in which her late spouse had died. Carlysle, she would have been the first to admit, was not a very lovable man. He wasn't handsome, even as a young man, and dying as he did at sixty, he'd become even less prepossessing. Nor was he fond of dogs or children, and on flag-flying days he was known to have looked the other way.

Wealthy he'd been, which was almost a natural consequence of his parsimonious, scheming lifetime, but even wealth didn't change him. He deplored Katherine's wastrel brother Edward, had belittled her defunct, rural-folk parentage and heritage, and in the end he had impressed Katherine with the same disposition, although because she was basically strong and God-fearing and honest, he hadn't made much headway in circumventing these nostalgic attributes although in attire, outlook, almost in conversation, she was like him.

When Detective Sergeant Lorillard, Francis Xavier Lorillard, formerly of the Boston, now of the Exeter Police Department, came by in response to Katherine's cryptic telephone call . . . 'My husband has been murdered, please send a policeman at once!' . . . he hadn't really expected to find a murdered man at all. Twenty-three years in the Force had taught Sergeant Lorillard two things. One of them was never to believe what a woman reporting a felony said over the telephone. The other one was never accept the judgement of uninitiated people concerning a corpse. For some reason, people did not ever come upon a dead person without at once announcing they had uncovered a murder. Someone breaking their neck stumbling downstairs in the dark, was invariably the victim of secret assailants. The composed heart-stoppage victim in his bed was said to have been poisoned. The red-faced stroke-victim found in a flower garden, clearly had been strangled by some mightily-muscled madman.

But Carlysle Stevens had two bullet holes in the back of his head, and aside from the extraordinary dexterity required for a person to hold up a gun at the base of the skull, it was unlikely that, maintaining this position once, the victim ever could have achieved it a second time. Both bullets exited through the forehead. Either one would have produced an instantaneous coma, and death.

So it was murder.

Not only had mousy Katherine Stevens been correct in her initial assessment, but she'd also reported it over the telephone in the precise, proper manner.

Furthermore, as though to douse a wound with liberal sprinklings of salt, while she and Sergeant Lorillard were viewing the corpse, on the floor of a cluttered little attic workshop, she further confounded things by stating emphatically that she had been in the downstairs dining-room polishing silver all morning, had heard no shots from the attic, and had seen no one go up the stairs, which were in plain view from where she'd been working.

In fact, Katherine's practicality made Lorillard view her askance. By her own admission she had been the only person in the house when the murder had to have been committed. She had seen nothing, had heard nothing, and was able now to stand in the narrow doorway of the attic workroom with her poor, late husband lying there as though napping, and knock the props out from under each theory Sergeant Lorillard had to consider, almost before he'd completed his preliminary investigation. And of course, whether Katherine was aware of it or not, she had talked herself squarely into position of Suspect Number One.

Except for a couple of minor details.

The gun was not found, which of

course didn't mean Katherine hadn't squirrelled it away, but both a blood-test and paraffin-test, patiently submitted to, failed to produce a solitary grain of gunpowder, or blood, on the hands and forearms of Katherine.

And no one Detective Sergeant Lorillard interviewed over the subsequent five days had so much as a breath of disparagement to breathe against Katherine, although not one of those people had much that was favourable to say about defunct Carlysle Stevens.

This in itself did not mean Katherine hadn't been nurturing in her somewhat ample bosom a flourishing hatred for the man who had kept her drab and penny-pinching all those years despite his wealth. It was in fact fairly common for women at a certain age to abruptly go off the deep end and kill husbands who had somehow failed to live up to their expectations, warranted or not.

Except that Doctor Harold Bradford, the town of Exeter's most valued citizen, renowned in medicine as well as psychiatry, and who lived alone next door in a most forbidding stone two-storied house, told Sergeant Lorillard in no uncertain terms it was nonsense and rubbish to suspect Katie Stevens of change-of-life aberrations.

'Absolutely asinine, Sergeant. In the first place Katie isn't that old. I *know* how she dresses; my gawd you don't have to remind me, after all I've lived next door for fifteen years. But she was almost twenty years younger than that old skinflint she married. Furthermore, please remember Katie Arnold Stevens is old New England stock. Her kind simply is not conditioned to murder. Look up the statistics, man; you'll find Yankee New Englanders have a much, much lower per-capita proportion of murderers among them than any other ethnic group.'

Francis Xavier Lorillard didn't look it up. Doctor Bradford may have been quite right; in fact Lorillard was perfectly amenable to the suggestion. Not simply because he was also of the old New England stock, but because he didn't give a Continental damn about ethnic propensities. He wanted a murderer, Yankee, Southerner, or whatever.

The way Carlysle Stevens had perished hadn't been exceptionally extraordinary. He'd had his back to the workshop door, had been bending over a workbench upon which he'd been turning a bed-bolster of hardwood upon his woodlathe. Someone had simply opened the door — evidently — aimed and fired.

It was always very difficult to say, with no more knowledge of what had occurred than Sergeant Lorillard possessed at the outset of his investigation, whether that second bullet had been a lucky hit, or whether the killer was so seasoned with a handgun that he — or she — could fire off the second round accurately while the dying man was moving, either springing upright, or perhaps going over against the workbench, preparatory to falling in a heap.

Whichever it was, the second bullet had struck within three inches of the first wound. Luck or not, it was a definitely lethal second shot.

Carlysle had fallen, of course, but he must have threshed a bit because he was several feet away from the base of the workbench, legs slightly drawn up, head turned sidewards, both arms loosely lying next to the body. In appearance old Stevens looked to be simply napping.

And the workshop door was closed.

The murderer had left, no doubt in haste, but he had had enough presence of mind to close the door after himself. Or after 'herself' as the case might be.

Also, despite the fact that the victim and his slayer couldn't have been separated by over eleven feet — Lorillard measured it on his hands and knees: Distance from door to workbench — both bullets had exited quite neatly, almost with surgical neatness, in fact.

By the time Lorillard got a sighting on trajectory and had dug one slug from the upper wall, the second slug from slightly lower down on the wall, where it had pierced the left eye of a painting of a Stevens ancestor hanging across the room, Lorillard could make a guess as to why Stevens's whole face hadn't been blown to bits by the exiting bullets. They were both heavily steel-jacketed; even slamming into skull-bone had failed to smash them. Only when they'd hit head-on into the ancient, gnarled old fir wood of the yonder wall had they pancaked.

He sent them down to Boston to the police laboratory. Exeter, with a population of ten thousand in the city, which was the County Seat, and another twenty-five thousand or so in the outlying rural districts, couldn't have paid for a police laboratory even if there'd been anyone in the county who could have operated it. Anyway, affairs like the Carlysle Stevens affair happened so very rarely — this was only the second murder in Exeter's history, which went back to the early French-and-Indian wars long before the American Rebellion — a crime-detection laboratory was hardly warranted.

That other murder, incidentally, had involved the lusty wife of a New Light minister whose scandalous carryings-on with a strapping big farmhand had led to the arsenically inspired expiration of the Reverend, and the subsequent confession, and holiday-hanging of the lusty widow and her enamoured lout.

That had happened shortly before the U.S. war with Mexico, and the great-grandfather of Carlysle Stevens had noted in his journal — subsequently burnt by Great Aunt Ophelia Stevens because of some heretical, profane, and outrageously salacious remarks — that the reverend's wife went to her death as a pure waste, for she was a very buxom and comely woman.

All that had happened in 1844. Since then there hadn't been a murder in Exeter, or the countryside either. For that reason Sergeant Lorillard expected a lot of well-meant advice to come, and he was not disappointed.

Even the *Exeter Clarion*, operated by a cliché-ridden, woefully pathetic intellectual eighty-year-old named Edgar Loose, who was actually well past forty although his 'Column', a daily source of asinine drivel, gave no hint that this was really Loose's age, came up with exactly the kind of 'Column' editorial Sergeant Lorillard might have expected. It said poor Carlysle Stevens, pillar of the community, scion of a great old New England family, had without question been killed by a sneak-thief who, having inadvertently encountered his victim in the course of burglarising the old Stevens mansion, had shot to prevent subsequent identification.

Unless Stevens had a third eye, not known to be a fact, then it did not seem too likely that he'd had any idea whatever that death was behind him, for he'd heard nothing at all, or, as Lorillard reasoned, he'd have turned, and then the bullets would have struck him in front.

But Loose's editorial was only a little more silly than some of the other theories people advanced, and Lorillard, a patient big man, resignedly listened simply because there was no way to keep from it.

Also, as he rationalised it, this was the first authentic murder in a hundred and twenty-seven years. It lent backwater Exeter, Massachusetts, a semblance of twentieth-century sophistication. It gave people something to argue about instead of the Vietnam war, which was getting to be a pretty threadbare topic anyway, and finally, it delighted the secret cockles of a lot of good New England hearts, because no one had liked Carlysle Stevens anyway.

2

Slow Progress

The primary disadvantage that pertains to any felon is that once a crime is committed, the criminal cannot go back and correct his mistakes, and that the police, not always possessed of any greater degree of intelligence than the criminal — very often not nearly as much — can take all the time they need, within reason, to unravel whatever has been left behind.

In big cities this more often than not contributes to the speedy solution of murders. In places no larger than Exeter, Massachusetts, it was ordinarily a great comfort to investigating officers, although in the case of the first clear-cut murder in over a century, this period of grace was, at least for Sergeant Lorillard, also filled with the verbal snipings of half the populace.

Even when he went forth to interrogate the friends of Mrs. Stevens or the business associates of the late defunct Carlysle Stevens, he was subjected to any number of carefully-deducted suggestions sure to lead to the apprehension of a two-legged monster.

For example, Joshua Brewster who operated Exeter's most thriving hardware store, a contemporary of Carlysle Stevens's, said that it was as plain as the nose on Sergeant Lorillard's face that Katherine's no-good brother Edward, had finally retaliated for the years of belittlement he'd had to endure from Katherine's husband.

Edward, it appeared, was a ne'er-do-well. Katherine, in her talk with Lorillard had not said that, but a number of other people, including Josh Brewster, had stated it as a fact.

But the two-legged monster Lorillard sought out, who lived in a dilapidated mansion on the edge of town which had once been the proud home of the Arnolds, was a sorry specimen of a monster indeed. Edward Arnold, a few years younger than his sister Katherine, was a lank, tousle-headed lantern-jawed Yankee with light blue eyes, a slovenly appearance, and a variety of almost fawning deference that indicated many years of belittlement and not just at the hands of Carlysle Stevens.

Edward had weak eyes, which Lorillard verified to his private satisfaction by asking Edward to read a legend beneath an old framed lithograph in the dirty parlour. Edward had first to rummage beneath heaps of old newspapers for some thick-lensed glasses.

Also, when Lorillard, a non-smoker, offered Edward a cigar, which was gratefully accepted, Edward's hands were not very steady.

Finally, Edward's mild, gentle disposition was the product of whatever environment had formed Edward, over a very long period of time. If there was even an ability in Edward Arnold to fly off the handle, it was buried so deeply beneath the layers of gentle conformity that without much question it was nearly non-existent.

So — Edward, with or without glasses, couldn't have been a good enough shot to have felled his brother-in-law the way Carlysle was done in. Nor were his hands steady enough to have delivered that second bullet. Ultimately, Edward, ne'er-do-well though he obviously was, simply had not the temperament for murder.

When Lorillard returned to the Stevens house to talk with Katherine about her brother, she sat primly gazing at him from her level, cornflower-blue eyes, shaking her head.

'Of all the possibles, Sergeant, you've picked the least. It is true Carlysle was contemptuous of my brother, and it was also true Edward avoided my husband if he could. But murder . . . ? Ridiculous. Edward has been deathly afraid of guns since childhood. Nor does he have the ability to hate anyone sufficiently to want to kill them. I guess you've heard what people say about poor Edward. The town jack-of-all-trades, handyman, mister fixit for stopped-up sinks, broken screendoors, leaky taps. Well; it's all true. Edward has been a dreamer all his life. It was a burden for my father — may he rest in peace — but then, Edward was simply Edward.'

Lorillard, wedged into a dainty little chair some long-forgotten Yankee captain had brought back in his sailing ship, considered Katherine's rather delicate but square-jawed face.

He smiled at her. 'Mrs. Stevens, I'm accumulating quite a respectable list of the ones who *couldn't have*, which of course would I suppose after a year or two, lead me to the ones who *could have*, but I don't believe I can wait that long to find the man who killed your husband. What I'd like would be a few names of people *you* think could have done it.'

'I've already told you, Sergeant, I have no idea at all. I told you that the first time you came to the house. Carlysle was not a man much admired, but as for murder — well — I can't feature who'd have done such a thing.'

It seemed to Lorillard that Mrs. Stevens equated murder with belching at prayer or some equally as unforgivable breach of decorum rather than as a grisly crime. He sighed.

'I've been going over your husband's business with the bank, Mrs. Stevens.' At the quick look of outrage this occasioned he said, 'I know it's not proper but then my job often demands improprieties of me.'

Her expression remained resentful.

'There was a man named Henry Winslow who owed Mr. Stevens some money on a parcel of land north of Exeter who is in arrears. Can you tell me anything about that?'

'Mr. Stevens did not confide his business affairs in me, Sergeant Lorillard.'

'But you knew Henry Winslow?'

'Yes.' Katherine's annoyed expression did not alter, and from now on her answers were minimal. 'I have known Henry Winslow all my life. We grew up here in Exeter, attended the same schools.'

'Well, that should give you some idea of the man's character, I would say, Mrs. Stevens.'

'Not at all.'

Sergeant Lorillard gazed steadily at

Mrs. Stevens. Her jaw was set, her stare was unyielding, until she'd overcome the annoyance he'd occasioned by saying he'd pried into her husband's affairs at the bank, there wouldn't be much point in continuing this discussion with her.

Lorillard arose. 'I'm sorry I've intruded,' he said. 'I'll call again. Good-day, Mrs. Stevens.'

She primly saw him to the door, bobbed her head and let him just barely clear the threshold before closing the door.

In another place, among a different variety of people, Lorillard would have been justified in thinking the widow's behaviour highly suspicious. But not in New England.

He went back to the bank and had another talk with Charles Dunston, Board Chairman of the Exeter Banking & Trust Company, the same person who had told him about Henry Winslow being in arrears to Carlysle Stevens on that land at the northerly edge of town.

Dunston, a paunchy man of impressive height and heft, was known throughout the countryside as a tough, knowledge-able banker, a man who knew more about other people's business affairs than anyone else in town, and also as a very realistic appraiser when it came to making loans.

Lorillard had known Charles Dunston since first coming to Exeter. At that time Dunston had been Police Commissioner; had in fact been largely instrumental in getting a retiring big-city detective to even consider coming to Exeter.

They were not close friends but they were congenial acquaintances, so when Lorillard walked in for his second interview, Charles Dunston held the chair for him, offered tea — it was mid-afternoon — then settled himself behind the massive black-oak desk that dominated his office and said, 'Well, how do you like Winslow for prime suspect, Sergeant?'

Lorillard smiled. He hadn't gone to see Winslow yet, but Dunston was the kind of person who would view this failure as an absolute dereliction, so Lorillard simply said, 'Bit early for sorting them out yet,

Mister Dunston. I was wondering if there was anyone else who might also have been in any financial difficulty with Carlysle Stevens?'

Dunston's little blue eyes shone with sudden recollection. 'Bless me, I'd almost forgot. George Macklin and Carlysle had a disagreement, but that's been several years ago.'

'Macklin?'

'Yes. He lives not very far from Edward Arnold's place. In fact they were friends. May still be for all I know. George was a lumberjack until liquor got the better of him after Mary-Beth, his wife, died six or seven years ago. Since then he's established a car-repair works out back of the house.'

'What was the disagreement about?'

Charles Dunston offered a bright, false smile. 'Money. Isn't that what all arguments are about, eh? Carlysle loaned George money for the funeral. The doctors had cleaned Macklin out during his wife's last illness. Afterwards, when George took to drink, Carlysle didn't like it. They had a disagreement.'

'Did Stevens get his money back?'

'Yes,' said Dunston. 'The bank undertook collection. I remember quite well that George was fairly prompt with his payments. I also recall him telling Carlysle right out there in front of half-dozen people, that if Carlysle didn't keep his long nose out of George's affairs, George would twist it right off his face.'

Sergeant Lorillard filed Macklin away in his mind and asked about other enemies of Carlysle Stevens, which elicited from Banker Dunston the comment that in Carlysle's sixty years, all of them spent right here in Exeter, and being the kind of person he was, Lorillard could find them all listed in alphabetical order, complete with addresses, simply by picking up the local telephone directory.

Later in the afternoon when Lorillard chanced to meet Doctor Harold Bradford out front of the County Court House, he got another slant on the Macklin matter. According to Doctor Bradford there had been a slight matter of unrequited love involved. 'Ask Katie,' he said. 'Her brother was in love with Mary-Beth before she married George Macklin, and afterwards as well.' Bradford furrowed his broad brow at Lorillard. 'Do you imagine that otherwise Carlysle would have lent a penny to Macklin? Of course not. George got Mary-Beth; Carlysle would have seen him rot in hell first.'

'Nothing quite like the background-material in a small town,' murmured Lorillard, and Doctor Bradford smiled.

'Sergeant, I've been in lots of 'em. Exeter's no different from the others except for one thing: Here, we have the classical dogmatism of our kind of people. I would want your job least of all, still, if I recall correctly, all the really great detectives have been English, have they not?'

Lorillard studied Doctor Bradford's kind, ruddy face for a sign of delicate sarcasm. 'Some difference,' he said, 'between Old English and New English, Doctor. As for the pity, save it for your suffering patients.'

'Quite. Well, Sergeant I wish you well in this investigation, and of course will be delighted to co-operate any way that I can.'

After they parted Sergeant Lorillard continued his stroll to the police station where his office, to the right of the main entrance and up one flight of old stone stairs, was cool in summer and downright cold in winter, but since this was spring, it now was rather pleasant.

Doctor Bradford, of old New England stock, could equate Lorillard's difficulties the same way others had done, by stressing the uncomplicated but fiercely stubborn character of the New Englanders Lorillard had to deal with, as opposed to the unlovely personality of the man who had been killed.

It did not dismay Lorillard. In fact if there had been a plain trail leading to the killer Lorillard would have felt immensely disappointed. It was that same endemic stubbornness in Lorillard, also a New Englander, which had made him a successful detective down in

Boston, and which kept him from feeling anything but a challenge now.

He could of course have assumed the mildly amused attitude of Doctor Bradford, or the faintly spiteful attitude of Banker Dunston, but in fact he was not very impressed with either attitude. He was interested in locating a murderer and whatever would be required of him until this were satisfactorily concluded, he would do without spite and without amusement.

Francis Xavier Lorillard only *looked* like a big, shambling St. Bernard of a man, and although he'd been employed as a detective by the township of Exeter for some little time prior to the Carlysle Stevens affair, he had not up until that time had to prove himself as being anything more than simply a man of brawn willing and able to arrest an occasional prowler, tyre-thief, obstreperous drinker.

As Edgar Loose, the intellectual cripple who operated Exeter's daily, and only, newspaper, said in his column, 'Detective Lorillard has his work cut out for him.' It was probably the only time Edgar Loose was correct in an editorial since predicting the election triumph of an unopposed incumbent Supervisor some years previously.

3

Katie's Revelation

Henry Winslow was a youngish man with sandy hair, brown eyes and a quiet manner. He lived in the eminently respectable section of Exeter in one of those two-storied traditional New England homes, left him by his parents, the last one of which, his mother, had died only the previous year.

Henry was quiet, wore thick-lensed glasses, was tall and lean and did not seem to Sergeant Lorillard as the kind of person to fly in the face of anyone.

Henry also had a forthright manner. When Lorillard mentioned the matter of delinquent payments to Carlysle Stevens, Winslow gave what seemed to be a very candid explanation.

'It is true, Sergeant, I was in arrears, and there was a slight dispute between us. Mister Stevens pointed out that by terms of the loan he could, if any payment became delinquent, demand the entire total plus interest within thirty days, and unless fully compensated, could foreclose.'

'Did he make that demand, Mister Winslow?'

'No sir.'

'And did you pay him off?'

'Eventually, yes, but it took a little more time. You see my mother, who finally died last year, was in her terminal illness at that time. The money I'd set aside to pay Mister Stevens went instead for her care.'

Lorillard pondered, then said. 'You paid Mister Stevens off in full, but took more time to do it, is that what you just said?'

Winslow nodded, polished his glasses, then he said, 'I make a little money from time to time buying pieces of outlying property, dividing them into lots and reselling them. It is fairly lucrative if I can get hold of parcels near the river, or up-country round one of the creeks or lakes.'

Lorillard was sure that it was lucrative and he couldn't possibly have cared less. On the drive back from the Winslow place he stopped off at George Macklin's garage. His car had been acting of late as though in need of retiming. It was his personal vehicle; Exeter did not furnish its detective with transportation — only its six-man uniformed police force.

George Macklin was a man as large and broad as Lorillard also was. He was slightly older than Lorillard but the weathering, the hard-living, the vocational vicissitudes which had shaped Macklin, made him seem quite a bit older.

Macklin was nobody's fool. When Lorillard alighted out back of Macklin's house where his auto-repair shop stood, to explain about the timing, Macklin softly smiled and said, 'I'll check the timing. There's an oscillascope inside the shop, Mister Lorillard, but that's not all that brought you out here is it?'

Lorillard smiled slightly. 'Not quite.'

They measured each other with a not-unfriendly interest, then Macklin went after his wheel-mounted motor-minder and boasted the bonnet of Lorillard's car as he said, 'You know, if I'd wanted to kill old Carlysle I'd never have needed a gun.'

Watching Macklin's huge hands at work Lorillard was inclined to agree but all he said was, 'Were you ever friendly with Stevens?'

Macklin bobbed his head with his back to Lorillard. 'Yes, years ago.' Macklin hooked the malfunctioning motor to his meter, turned and watched the needles. Afterwards, removing the connections he said, 'You need a tune-up, Sergeant. New points, spark-plugs, probably a new coil and condenser as well. After all, the car's not new.'

Lorillard agreed that the car was not new. He asked if Macklin had the time right now to take care of him. Macklin nodded and went to work. After that their conversation was sporadic and frequently interrupted when Macklin revved the motor or leaned far beneath the bonnet, practically out of sight.

When the car was finished, purred

properly and Lorillard was paying Macklin, the former lumberjack said with an expression of amiability, 'Sergeant, there's more to the story than me tellin' Carlysle to keep his beak out of my affairs.'

Lorillard nodded. He'd already heard there was more. He assumed that now Macklin's version of Carlysle's unrequited love would come out. But it didn't. Macklin said, 'Ask Katie,' and went to put the money Lorillard had handed him in the cash-drawer. Then he waved through the window at Lorillard and walked away, deeper into his shop where other cars waited.

Lorillard wasn't eager to get back to the Stevens place. Still, it had been a couple of days; it seemed unlikely Katherine would still be annoyed at him.

She wasn't, but when she admitted him to the parlour she was not very talkative either. However, that was a New England characteristic, as well as the possible result of Lorillard's indiscretion at the bank, so he became hopeful when she asked if he'd care for tea.

He loathed the stuff. 'It would be just exactly right,' he assured her, and when it came he drank it with feigned smile of contentment.

'You'll be wanting to talk about my husband and Mary-Beth Macklin, I expect,' she said to him, and at his quiet stare she said, 'You'd be coming to that sooner or later, Sergeant. It just happened to be sooner.'

Her gaze did not falter, but neither was it challenging nor defiant. She looked Lorillard squarely in the eye as she spoke, and her voice was crisp and matter-of-fact. It was difficult to imagine anyone but a New Englander discussing something as charged with personal emotion as a husband's old love with a near-stranger, without batting an eye or faltering in the recitation.

'I have no idea when it first happened, Sergeant, but my husband was very fond of Mary-Beth.'

'Before or after his marriage, Mrs. Stevens?'

'I should think both, Sergeant.' The level Yankee eyes were thoughtful. 'I think a man only really has one great love in his lifetime, Sergeant. It needn't be his wife, and it probably can come to him long after he's married. Of course it's not obligatory that he do anything about it. Carlysle didn't. He wouldn't have in any case; it just wasn't his nature to be demonstrative.'

Lorillard soberly nodded. New Englanders may have been regarded as uncomplicated, somewhat stolid people, but as far as Lorillard's work was concerned it might have helped somewhat if they'd also been a little less inhibited.

Still, he understood what Mrs. Stevens was telling him, which a less compatible detective might not have understood at all.

He asked if Katherine knew much about the ill-will between her husband and George Macklin. She smiled. 'Carlysle made two suggestions to George. I happened to be present both times. The first suggestion was that

George stop drinking.'

'I see. After his wife's death.'

'No, Sergeant. Charley Dunston didn't tell it to you correctly. *Before* his wife's death.'

Lorillard blinked. Why had she said Charles Dunston had told him? Then she spoke on and he didn't have an opportunity right then to explore this other matter.

'The second suggestion was that George make up his mind that with Mary-Beth failing, he could not return to the north woods but would have to undertake some gainful employment right here in Exeter so he could be close when she'd need him.'

Lorillard, thinking back to his visit with Macklin, decided that the former-woodsman was indeed the kind of person who would articulately resent this variety of advice. But was it enough to drive Macklin to murder?

Not to Lorillard's way of thinking it wasn't.

He fidgeted on the chair and Katie asked if he'd like more tea. He could gracefully decline so he did so. Then he said, 'You mentioned Mister Dunston . . . ?'

Her smile returned, soft and wise. 'Sergeant, Charley Dunston is the town busybody. You would go to him, of course, and although it irritated me the other day, I realise now it's different with you — your job requires you to do things like that. I also realised what Charley would tell you. After all, I grew up with Charley. I've known him all his life. He was a snoopy little boy, an obnoxiously prying young man, and now, as town-banker, he exults in knowing everyone's personal as well as financial affairs. That's why I said what I did.'

'Mister Dunston didn't mention Macklin drinking *before* his wife died. Only after.'

Katie's small smile lingered. 'Sergeant, you've met George Macklin. Would you say he would be likely to storm into a bank and perhaps make a scene if he learned someone in the bank had been telling tales about him to a policeman?'

Lorillard smiled back at Katie. 'I think

he might do that, yes.'

'Then you have the answer to why Charley was discreet with you about George Macklin.'

'One more question then I'll go, Mrs. Stevens: Did your husband resent Macklin's treatment of his wife?'

Katherine shook her head. 'No, Sergeant. Why would he? George deeply loved Mary-Beth. Drinking or sober he was very sweet to her. If you're thinking that because George was a woodsman; a rough, profane man, big and sometimes a bit troublesome, especially on Saturday nights, you will be correct. But he was gentle as a child with Mary-Beth. Carlysle said so several times.'

'Said what?'

'That George was a good husband.'

Lorillard arose. It was a sunshiny day beyond the shadowy old parlour. Katherine's petunias were coming into the first multi-coloured bloom and her tea-roses, which lined the walk from street to porch, were showing fat buds. There were noisy birds in the elms and sycamores that shaded both house and grounds.

'Thank you,' said Lorillard, and let her take him to the front entry-hall where a gilt-framed ancestor with mutton-chop whiskers and wearing a blue uniform, looked down with steely eyes from a papered wall. She saw him gaze briefly at the ancestor and said it was her late husband's grandfather, who had been an officer of the Second Massachusetts' Infantry, Grand Army of the Republic. Then she said something that startled Sergeant Lorillard.

'You know how it is, Mister Lorillard; New Englanders always talk proudly of their Yankee-clipper sea-captains, but by themselves they are more proud of their grandfathers for whipping the Southern Confederacy. But as you may have deduced from my maiden name, neither my brother nor I have any reason to discuss soldier-ancestors.'

He looked up with slow comprehension. The name she'd implied rang instantly in his memory. Every New Englander, in fact every American, could recall it without a moment's hesitation. But he didn't mention it aloud. She did.

'General Arnold.'

Lorillard didn't know whether to commiserate or to attempt some weak defence of America's most notorious traitor. He covered his confusion by looking at his watch.

Katie opened the door, her blue eyes dark with soft irony. 'Do come again,' she said, and smiled. 'I'd have thought surely Charley Dunston would have told you that straightaway, Sergeant. When Edward and I were children he used to tease us about it day in and day out.'

Lorillard said a little lamely, 'Well, but that's been nearly two hundred years ago.'

With practical New England forthrightness Katie said, 'Judas got his pieces of silver even longer ago and people still talk about it, Sergeant.'

Lorillard was driving back to his office, still amazed at Katherine's revelation about her family, when the sun sank and he was obliged to recognise that this day was nearing its end. He kept a room at the Exeter Hotel, had taken it when he'd first arrived in town and had seen no reason to move afterwards, so after a brief stop at the police station, he went to the hotel for a bath, a change, and dinner downstairs in the dining-room where he also had a highball at the small bar.

It was a pleasant evening, not chilly as most springtime New England evenings were, and after dinner Sergeant Lorillard went out onto the large, deep front porch of the hotel to fire up his pipe and sit in the shadows where one could watch the strollers, or where one could simply ruminate.

He did both, but the more he thought the less he noticed people, and shortly before he heaved up out of the chair to head for his room and bed, it occurred to him that perhaps poor Edward had more reason than just his personal inabilities to be as deferential and diffident as he was.

But that didn't add up to a murder either, so, when Lorillard hiked up the stairs to his room, he had to admit that he had no more, now, than he'd had the day of Carlysle Stevens's passing, to help him find a murderer.

4

A New Riddle

Joshua Brewster, owner and operator of Exeter's most prosperous hardware store, was a wizened man with weak, very pale eyes behind tortoise-shell glasses of considerable vintage. He reminded Lorillard of a sprite; a bird-like individual whose jerky movements and quick, probing glances pierced through to each customer's bank balance.

Joshua's ancestors had arrived in New England later than the Puritans, but not much later, and there had been several of them who became prominent about the time George III assumed his stubborn attitude towards the American Colonies.

It wasn't hard to look at Joshua Brewster now and visualise those other Brewsters. They may have been different in appearance but Lorillard thought it likely they'd possessed the same sharp minds and facile tongues.

It was Brewster whose references to other people had sent Lorillard out to interview Edward Arnold, among others, so the moment he entered the store Joshua turned a customer over to one of his three clerks and fairly skipped up to ask if Lorillard had made an arrest yet.

The answer was mildly given. 'No. All things in good time, Mister Brewster.'

Joshua's look of disappointment was such that no amount of control could have hidden it entirely. 'But by now you'll have someone in mind, surely.'

Lorillard smiled. 'Half the town I'm afraid, but the jail isn't that big so I'll have to keep on narrowing it down.'

'People are impatient, Sergeant.'

If that was a warning it slid off Lorillard's wide shoulders. 'Maybe these people you mention would prefer to handle the case without me, Mister Brewster.'

That stung Joshua into backing up a little. 'Only a figure of speech, of course.'

'Of course,' agreed Lorillard, who loomed above the sprite-like smaller man.

'You grew up here in Exeter didn't you, Mister Brewster?'

'Aye. Seventh or eighth generation, I forget which.'

'And you knew Carlysle Stevens.'

'Very well. Better than most, I'd say, seeing as how we were about the same age, attended school together, had a few dealings now and again.'

Lorillard, driving towards what those last words implied, asked another question, 'Was he always disliked; I mean, as a young man, as a child?'

Joshua Brewster's little pale eyes glinted behind their glass windows. 'I think you're a lot less dense than that fool who runs the newspaper has been hinting, Sergeant. No, as a matter of fact, 'Lysle Stevens was not disliked as a child. Nor as a young man, although it was about that time . . . I'd say when 'Lysle started making money which would be when he was in his late twenties . . . that he became objectionably outspoken. After that, he made enemies. When he eventually married Katie Arnold, he'd got to the point where people shunned him. He was never a man needful of a lot of friends anyway.

'One time, long ago, I borrowed two thousand dollars from 'Lysle Stevens. It was during the Depression and the store was in bad shape — no trade, lots of uncollectable accounts, inventory 'way down. I caught the appendicitis. Couldn't pay a clerk so had to close the store for three weeks until I could get back on my feet. 'Lysle lent me the money, but it took a long while to pay him back, you understand, and he'd drop round once a day — at noon by that Seth Thomas clock on the wall — and glare at me.'

'Did you pay him back?'

'Yes — with interest.' Brewster made a slow, sly smile. 'I think 'Lysle regretted that I could pay him off.'

'Because he wanted to foreclose and own your store?'

'Oh no. Because he couldn't come round every day and glare at me from the doorway.'

Lorillard bought a tin of pipe tobacco, made a slow, thoughtful survey of the laden shelves, the oiled old puncheon floor, the general, antiquated look of the showcases and said, 'Did this business come to you from relatives, Mister Brewster?'

'Aye. Believe it or not, Sergeant, my grandfather founded it before The War.'

'Would that be the *Civil* War, Mister Brewster?'

'Yes indeed. Before that the Brewsters were farmers.'

Lorillard pocketed the tin of tobacco — he didn't have a pipe with him, very rarely ever carried one or smoked during the day — gazed out into the sun-bright street through shiny glass windows that had interesting waves in them that distorted things viewed through them, and could almost see the thinned ranks of the Second Massachusetts swinging through the sunshine out there, fifes riffling, drums rolling, faded blue uniforms showing below the flinty, uncompromising faces of dour New Englanders.

'Time was,' piped up Joshua Brewster, 'people said 'Lysle Stevens would run the bank.'

That brought Lorillard back to the present. 'Did he want to run it, Mister Brewster?'

'No. If he'd wanted to he could have. Before Charley Dunston took over there was Ben Carlock managing. Ben died and 'Lysle, folks said, being biggest shareholder, would step in. He didn't. Once I asked him, and he said a man with an ounce of gumption to him should aspire to something better than sitting behind a desk all day with a tie knotted like a damned noose round his gullet.'

Brewster chirped up in bird-like laughter and slapped his leg. Sergeant Lorillard stoically stood gazing at him, showing no signs of reciprocal amusement. Brewster throttled his neighing and said, 'Well, 'Lysle went and bought that woodworking equipment and installed it up in his attic, and isn't that even sillier than sitting behind a desk in a bank?'

Lorillard didn't know whether it was or not. He said, 'Did Mister Stevens and Charles Dunston get on well?'

Brewster was sure they had; at least

he'd never heard either of them disparage the other, and when he'd seen them meet on the street they were cordial to one another.

Lorillard left the store shortly before noon, went up to a little restaurant he infrequently patronised for lunch, and afterwards drifted on over to his office, where the ballistics report from the Boston Police Department laboratory was waiting.

The pair of bullets dug out of the attic wall by Lorillard and forwarded for identification, said the report, had been fired from a Luger pistol, vintage Second World War.

That was a great help; next to those coal-scuttle German helmets, every U.S. soldier had tried hardest to bring home a German Luger pistol as a souvenir. There were undoubtedly thousands of them in Massachusetts, and of that number probably not more than a double handful had ever been registered with the police. Souvenir-pistols in boxes in attics were mostly forgotten even by the men, paunchy now and grey, who had brought them home so long ago.

Lorillard was delving into his desk-drawer for his pipe when the next paragraph of the ballistics report stopped him stone-still.

The bullets that had killed Carlysle Stevens had been fired from a Colt automatic .32 calibre pistol.

Lorillard forgot about the pipe, took the report to the only window in his office and re-read it. The wording came out the same that time too. In its laconic style the report said there was no connection between the Luger slugs sent for analysis, and the Coroner's report as forwarded by Doctor Harold Bradford for routine examination by the Boston authorities. Furthermore, in case there was any doubt, tests for bone, blood or meat fragments had failed completely, although other tests showed some particles of rust and decaying wood-dust, meaning that the Luger bullets had probably been in the attic wall for some time; perhaps years.

Sergeant Lorillard took the report back to the desk, sank down and made a final close study of it. In the end, troubled though he couldn't help but feel, at least there was no sense of frustration because as yet he had no preconceived ideas about the murder — although he most certainly *did* have one about the victim.

But that private opinion only complicated things.

He drove back to the Stevens' place, found Katie weeding a flowerbed out back, and accompanied her to a shaded porch while she shed her gardening gloves and pushed back a thick wave of brown hair that had tumbled across her wide forehead.

He asked about guns in the house. She knew of two, both rifles, both left over from military service by her husband's predecessors. They were kept in a closet and when she took Lorillard to see them, he discovered that one was indeed an ancestral piece. In fact it was one of those long, delicate Pennsylvania rifles commonly called a 'Kentucky' rifle and used during the American Rebellion. It not only hadn't been fired but it was doubtful if there was anyone around who'd even know how to load and charge the thing. Also, it had a layer of musty dust thick enough to use for powder.

The other weapon was a stubby little government-issue Springfield carbine of the variety given horse-soldiers in the early phases of the U.S. Civil War. It was also layered over with dust and hadn't been fired, although it was more amenable to modern use, being a breechloader. There were two difficulties though, one was that acquiring the proper ammunition would be hard, and the second difficulty was simply that as great as was the pig of lead one of those pieces used, if Carlysle had been shot with this weapon it would have splattered his head all over the room.

Lorillard put the weapons back, wiped his hands upon a handkerchief, thanked Katie, then asked about pistols. There were none, she was quite sure. Her husband had not liked the idea of having firearms about.

He asked if they might go to the attic. She led the way with a strong step and a sturdy resolution. When he showed her the places where he'd dug out the Luger bullets she looked utterly blank.

He explained about the weapon that had fired those slugs and she simply looked at him and said, 'How could that be, Sergeant? My husband had no such gun, nor would he have allowed anyone to shoot one in the house.'

'Have you always lived here? Couldn't someone have perhaps rented the place or — ?'

'Sergeant, my husband's people *built* this house. Only Stevenses have lived here since before the Rebellion. What you say means this German pistol couldn't have been more than perhaps a generation old.'

'That is right.'

She shook her head most emphatically. 'It couldn't have been fired here within the past twenty-five years.'

Lorillard said softly, 'Madam, it most certainly *was* fired there within that period. Those are the bulletholes. I dug out the slugs myself.'

They returned to the parlour. Katie said she'd make tea. Sergeant Lorillard absently assented, then went to stand at a curtained parlour window gazing out into the lovely old shady garden until she returned with the tray, and only then did he realise what he'd committed himself to.

But he drank the stuff, and Katie, whose mind had been busy in the kitchen, now said, 'The bullets were there; we accept that. But how did they *get* there?'

Lorillard had several theories but he advanced none of them. He finished the tea manfully, gazed at sturdy Katie and tried to be hopeful about finding a different pistol — a Colt .32 calibre automatic.

He did not tell her about the ballistics report because there was no real point in it; she knew of no guns in the house, that was quite clear, and anyway the impersonal wording of the report hadn't been designed to make the widow of a murder victim serene in mind.

He thanked her for the tea and she accompanied him as far as the front porch this time, something she'd never done before. It was while he was standing down two stairs and while she was still on the porch, that she said, 'Sergeant, could someone have been hiding up there in the attic waiting for Carlysle?'

That possibility had occurred to Lorillard shortly after he'd visited the attic that first time, while the corpse was still lying on the floor. The reason he'd rejected it wouldn't sound very valid — because the door had been closed from the outside — so all he answered was something to the effect that he wouldn't rule that out, but neither would be very inclined to reply upon it as his sole basis for finding her husband's killer.

After that they parted. Lorillard returned to his office and sat studying the ballistics report almost until quitting time, and instead of finding any clue in the written pages, he found instead only a deepening mystery.

5

An Excursion Into the Past

There were any number of advantages to being a detective in a large city, as opposed to holding the same position in a place no larger than Exeter, Massachusetts, and one of them was the ability to step into an adjoining office and use some other detective as one's testing-plank.

For Lorillard, who was the only plainclothes officer on the Exeter police force, there was nothing other than six uniformed patrolmen to go over his murder case with, and they, like the balance of the citizenry, already had their minds made up. In fact the lieutenant, a beefy, red-faced, gravel-throated individual named Grady, said that in his opinion it was a burglar who'd killed old Stevens and regardless of what anyone ever said, he'd remain convinced.

Edgar Loose continued to editorialise

and the fact that he had never once interviewed Lorillard, knew none of the really salient facts of the case, did not stop him from having an opinion. Wrong of course, but Loose was a man with an enormous ego; that would prevent him from candidly admitting he knew nothing.

Lorillard was eating a late dinner at the hotel when Doctor Bradford, coming downstairs after tending a patient, spied him and came to the table. Lorillard offered a greeting and a chair. He'd had no idea the doctor would take the chair but he did. He also ordered a double Scotch and soda, pulled out a spare chair for his black bag, then leaned back and said, 'My mother wanted me to enter the ministry, my father thought there was greater political opportunity in the law. So I had to hit a medium, and chose medicine. Which may prove, Sergeant, that a man just may be born with poor judgement.'

The double Scotch came, Doctor Bradford sipped it, studied Lorillard and said, 'Well, what progress, Sergeant, or has this murderer got quite away?'

Lorillard finished his dinner, leaned and reached for the coffee cup. 'He may have got away, Doctor, but I doubt very much that he even tried.'

'Ah? Then you don't subscribe to the local theory of inadvertent murder committed by a burglar.'

'It's possible,' smiled Lorillard. 'About the only theory I never cared for was that one about suicide.'

Bradford chuckled. 'Loose; well, no one really pays him much mind.'

'I got back the ballistics report, Doctor. It says Stevens was killed by .32 calibre slugs fired from a Colt automatic.'

'Interesting, Sergeant,' murmured Bradford, then topped off his drink and shoved the glass away. 'Seems to be endemic in the neighbourhood. That old house behind the Stevens place on the adjoining square belonged to a man named Carlock who was at one time, I believe, connected with our local banking establishment. He killed himself quite a few years ago.'

Lorillard had heard that Carlock had

died, not that he'd committed suicide. Of course one necessarily followed the other but ordinarily people mentioned suicide, not just the fact of death.

Seeking more information Lorillard said, 'Is that so?'

Bradford nodded. 'I wasn't in town at the time — up-state doing some refresher work. Carlock had something incurable — I'm hazy on that too although it seems I was told it was terminal lymph imbalance. At any rate he was bed-ridden for a while, then upped and blew his brains out. Everyone was properly shocked, of course. New Englanders don't do things like that.' Bradford smiled.

Afterwards, when Doctor Bradford had resumed his way homeward, fuelled to make it non-stop after his sojourn in the dining-room with Lorillard, hotel activity dwindled.

There were always a few town-couples who ate-out, as they called it, just for the change, but these people rarely lingered. By the time Lorillard went out to have his nightly smoke on the front porch, the lobby was quietly empty, lights in the dining-room had been dimmed, and upstairs the hotel's residents, permanent and transient, were getting ready to retire.

Lorillard wasn't tired nor sleepy so he sat and puffed and casually reflected on the town, its people, its past and present. He made no excursions into his imagination regarding its future. Lorillard was not given to flights of fancy.

What Harold Bradford had told him was food for thought, although perhaps not in any related context to what was presently uppermost in his mind. He smiled to himself: How the townsfolk must have whispered over that ill man's suicide. Deplorable, it was, by New England standards. A sure sign of moral weakness. He could imagine the ministers in their Sunday pulpits make oblique references to it and warning their congregations that Man was not entitled to destroy himself.

It was just such rubbish as this that had kept pragmatic Francis Xavier Lorillard from being a strong churchman. For more than twenty years he'd had a solid conviction that it wasn't God's will, but was rather Man's stubbornness, that had perpetuated antiquated tenets such as the one withholding from those dying in prolonged agony the right of relief and escape.

As for the dead man, Ben Carlock, he would be by now all but forgotten. As Lorillard arose to step up and knock out his pipe on the railing, he wondered how many other suicides there'd been in Exeter, that had been discreetly hushed-up or concealed. It was one of the fringe-benefits of Yankee bull-headedness to be a little hypocritical.

Lorillard retired to his room, lay awake for a while in the springtime chill of a moonless night, and finally fell asleep.

The following morning, still pondering the taking-off of Dunston's predecessor at the bank, Lorillard by-passed his office and drove directly to the Stevens' place. Katie, he knew, would be up and stirring; early-rising was another Yankee virtue.

He was correct. She greeted him at the door with a little smile and an offer of coffee and eggs. He accepted the offer of coffee, then, while she was preparing it in the kitchen he hiked up to the attic workshop and stood by the solitary transom window for a bit.

Later, recounting Doctor Bradford's conversation of the evening before, he saw Katie's expression turn grave. She had known the Carlocks quite well, she told him. After Mister Carlock's passing his wife and daughter had left Exeter. Katie had lost track of them over the years, which was reasonable since the daughter would by this time be a woman as old as Katie was, doubtless married long since and with a family of her own.

As for Ben Carlock, he had indeed killed himself. It had shocked the town although at the time he'd been out of the bank almost two years and was seldom seen outside his house, so people could scarcely feel much personal regard one way or another. It was, Katie said — and Lorillard smiled into his coffee cup — simply that suicide wasn't a very nice word.

Lorillard went round to the old

two-storey house later, promising Katie he'd return, and the present owner, an arthritic former mill-worker from over at Skenesboro named Pendelton, who operated the old mansion as a rooming-house, let Lorillard look about. The upstairs rooms were presently without occupants, so Lorillard had no interruptions in his prowlings.

When he'd finished, had extricated himself from the garrulous company of the landlord, and ambled back round to the Stevens' place, he had a theory. He tried it out on Katie.

Upstairs, in the attic workshop, he showed her the transom window, which was in line with three windows across the way in the former Carlock residence. Those three rooms were bedrooms. They had, he thought, also been bedrooms during the Carlock tenure.

'Now then; I'll have to determine what kind of weapon Mister Carlock shot himself with. But if it was a Luger pistol, then I may be correct in assuming that it was bullets from that gun I dug out of the wall here.'

Katie was sceptical. 'Would he have fired two of them?'

Lorillard smiled patiently. He'd already thought on that. 'One, we'll presume, to test the weapon. The second into himself, possibly, or maybe he fired *two* out of the window to test the weapon. I'm speculating you understand.'

She looked slowly from the window to Lorillard. 'About twenty years ago, Sergeant, I do recall my husband being upset over birds flying into this window and breaking it. He replaced the panes.'

Lorillard nodded. 'If you'd like, I'll let you know later on what I turn up.'

She said she would be very interested, and saw him out.

He went directly to the Court House, dug into old files for the Carlock certificate of death, which referred him to a Coroner's report, which in turn sent him to the storeroom in the cellar of the building where he found Exhibit A — a German Luger pistol.

At the time of Carlock's suicide the pistol must have only very recently been brought home by some local soldier. In fact, preserved by an oily rag, the gun was still in excellent condition.

Lorillard put the weapon back in its box, left the store-room, returned to his office where he noted the serial number of the suicide-gun on a scrap of paper, then he went down the street to a little café for luncheon.

The mystery of the two slugs he'd dug out of the attic wall, as well as the erroneous theory about birds flying into the attic window, breaking it, had been solved.

He finished eating and drove back to the Stevens' place to tell Katie what he'd discovered. She was interested. Also, she was wearing a very becoming beige dress that observant Sergeant Lorillard did not actually believe was a house dress, and she had her wealth of brown hair brushed until it shone.

She shed one little ray of light on the German pistol, too, finally. 'Daphne, the Carlock's daughter, was at that time going with a young man. You know him, Sergeant. Henry Winslow.'

Lorillard nodded. He did indeed know Henry Winslow.

'He had been home from the war only a few months when Mister Carlock killed himself.'

Lorillard tucked that scrap of intelligence away in his mind for future reference; it could very probably account for how Carlock got the German pistol. He suggested as much and Katie concurred. Then she smiled and said, 'I'm glad that's solved, Sergeant. You were so sure — and I was just as sure you had to be wrong.' She arose, smoothed her dress and suggested tea. He sat looking at her. She was indeed a fine figure of a woman. But he still did not like tea so he said it was a bit soon after lunch, then he rescued her from having to stand there looking expectant by saying he thought he ought to go see Henry Winslow to verify their theory.

She went with him to the door, looking thoughtful. As he stepped forth upon the porch she said, 'Sergeant, I bought a large roast yesterday — I don't know what I was thinking about because it's much too large for one person . . . ' She kept looking up into his face.

'It would be nice if you'd come back for supper.'

He hesitated but only out of habit. He'd made up his mind the moment she'd extended the invitation. 'It would put you to a lot of unnecessary trouble, Mrs. Stevens.'

'It would be a pleasure, Sergeant. It's been such a long time since I cooked for a man who could do justice to a meal. My father was a large man, like you, and when he sat down to the supper table he ate.'

Lorillard gently smiled — and held some uncharitable thoughts about defunct Carlysle Stevens. 'If you're sure it wouldn't be too much trouble, I'll confess to being awfully tired of hotel cooking.'

Her eyes brightened with a quicksilver softness. 'Seven o'clock?'

'Thank you, Mrs. Stevens,' he said, and departed.

On the drive to the old Winslow place

he pondered on the advisability of encouraging a friendship with the widow Stevens. On any metropolitan police force he'd ever heard of such carryings-on would not be approved of at all. But Exeter was not a city and the police force was not so professional.

And he really *was* tired of hotel cooking.

When he found Henry Winslow the lanky, frail bachelor was going over some topographical charts on his diningroom table. Lorillard came directly to the point, and at once saw that he'd struck a nerve when the German pistol was mentioned.

Winslow made no denial. In fact, as he poured out his story he seemed almost relieved to be talking about it.

'I brought the gun home as a souvenir. I didn't give it Mister Carlock, I simply left it there for him to look at — something from the war, Sergeant. Do you understand?'

'Yes. And . . . ?'

Winslow shrugged. 'Daphne and I went for a drive. We were engaged, you see.

When he returned, rather late that night . . .'

'He had killed himself?'

'Yes . . . A month later the widow and daughter left Exeter. I've never heard from Daphne since.' Winslow's eyes lingered upon Lorillard's face. 'I suppose her attitude was understandable. I had left her father with the weapon he killed himself with.'

Lorillard left Henry Winslow as discreetly as he could.

6

An Evening With Katie

The days appeared to be getting a little longer. At least by the time Lorillard had finished dressing for his dinner engagement the sun was still distantly visible upon the feathery ridge of a distant mountain, and shadows had made very little progress against the light.

He stood a moment, big hands loosely clasped behind his back gazing from the upstairs window out over Exeter's roof-tops, a thick giant of a man, gentle of feature and calm of eye, reflecting on how little some New England towns ever seemed to change.

Granted, Exeter was off the beaten path, and granted too there was neither industry nor expanding commerce to draw outlanders, Exeter should have shown *some* signs of growth if for no other reason than simply because the national population was expanding.

But the town wasn't even on a sea coast nor a river, which a good many New England towns were, so summer-people scarcely made a ripple either. True, there were the misty mountains not too distant, lures for autumn hunters, but these hardy souls were never numerous; fall and winter in Massachusetts were more than a period of reddening leaves and plummeting temperature. They were also times of icy winds out of the North, lashing rainstorms and brittle cold that could become, just overnight, so intense knuckles, knees, finger-joints, functioned only with pain and effort.

Lorillard had been any number of different places. Bermuda, for example, where trade-breezes kept the land delightfully sparkling year-round. Or Florida, glittering with opulence on its Gold Coast, likewise blessed year-round. But he was a born-and-bred New Englander. He always returned, even when he wondered about that himself.

He watched a shadow form on the lee side of a gaunt church steeple, and smiled. A man, he thought, was both formed and sustained by something called 'environment' and he could no more escape it than he could soar to the heavens unaided. What made that worth smiling over was that all the breathless cries for total freedom, total emancipation, were foolish; a man was never free and could never be free.

With that resolved to his quiet satisfaction, Lorillard went down to his car, neglected to set the odometer — he was paid ten cents a mile for using his own car in an official capacity, which he was not now doing — and drove leisurely out through town to the residential neighbourhood where Katie lived, parked in front of the walk and strode to the porch.

She opened the door as he reached for the old-fashioned bell-twist, smiling and amazingly transformed. He blinked in spite of himself.

Her gown was not the usual nondescript sheath he'd always seen her dressed in before, and her eyes seemed larger, more calm and warm than before because of the face make-up she had on now — ever so lightly it was true, but nonetheless make-up. Her hair, softly shining, thick and wavy, was formed to frame her face, which it did very well.

Katie was no budding girl. She was sturdily and amply made, Lorillard had noticed that at their first meeting, but tonight she seemed different in that respect too. Lorillard, however declined to speculate very much about that as he greeted her, stepped indoors and let her lead him to the parlour. He instead thought about the *total* change and decided that Carlysle Stevens had been blind to keep his wife looking as drab and shapeless as she'd seemed the first time Lorillard had ever seen her.

She asked about Henry Winslow. Lorillard had to think a minute before answering. 'It was his gun. He left it for Carlock to look at. He took Carlock's daughter out. They were engaged. When they returned Carlock had killed himself.'

'Yes,' said Katie, 'how sad,' and for ten seconds they sat a little awkwardly looking at one another because Katie didn't keep the conversation going.

Lorillard had the knack. After all, his profession required an ability to put people at their ease; to talk to men and women he'd never seen before as though they'd been acquainted a long while. He said, 'The whole thing is in the courthouse files, even to the Death Certificate. I was wondering whether your husband and Mister Carlock were friends.'

Katie thought they might have been but wasn't sure. 'He mentioned him a few times but if they were very close it must have been prior to our marriage. He died very shortly afterwards you know.'

Something suddenly came to Lorillard's mind. He sat a moment in silence and when Katie excused herself to go look at the oven, Lorillard arose, strode to a window and stood gazing out into the settling night.

It seemed that Harold Bradford, in casually touching upon the Carlock tragedy, had told Lorillard he'd been upstate doing some kind of academic work at the time of Carlock's death. And yet the signature on Carlock's Certificate of Death, bold as brass, was 'Harold Bradford, M.D.'

Katie came to say supper was ready. When Lorillard turned he could tell from her solemn expression she didn't think the evening was going quite as it should, or perhaps as she'd hoped it might. He resolved to see that she was not disappointed.

As he held her chair in the gloomy old oaken diningroom he said, 'You look especially pretty tonight, Mrs. Stevens,' then, as she smiled over at him where he was drawing forth his own chair, he said, 'That sounded like I was talking to some elderly aunt. I should have said, you're very pretty tonight, Katie.'

She blushed.

The roast was cooked to perfection, well-done on the outside, moderately rare deeper down. The potatoes too were rich and creamy. Lorillard wondered at the calories and when he tasted the coffee, made strong in the traditional New England manner, he wondered if that were an accident or if she'd deduced that he did not care much for tea.

She said quietly that Carlysle hadn't been much of an eater. 'Pecked at his food. Always had something else on his mind. As I told you, Sergeant, I came of rural stock; nothing can be as discouraging to a country woman as to cook a big meal, then have a man pick at it.'

With that inadvertent admonition, Lorillard had another slice of well-done meat and a second cup of coffee. Then he said, 'You would know a lot more about Mister Stevens than I would, naturally, and yet despite all I hear, he doesn't come across to me quite true to form.'

Katie sat in the soft light gazing at Lorillard. She said, her blue eyes stone steady and soft, 'Doesn't he?'

Lorillard thought she was mocking him. He said, 'It's always difficult to reconstruct things, particularly personalities, when you've never actually known the person. And in this instance I'm probably wrong.'

She showed her gentle small smile. 'Sergeant, I wouldn't imagine you are wrong very often. My impression of you is of a quiet, thoughtful, shrewd man who hides a very sharp capacity for perception behind a bear-like exterior.'

Lorillard laughed. 'That's protective colouration, Katie. The only truly perceptive detective I ever heard of was Sherlock Holmes. All others are simply persistent. That includes me.'

'Am I entitled to ask, Sergeant, if by now you have some inkling about Carlysle's murder?'

'If you mean do I suspect anyone in particular, the answer is — no. But if you mean have I uncovered anything of interest, I'd have to say quite a bit.' He smiled at her. 'But none of it as far as I can see now, has much bearing on what happened to your husband. For example, you are a wonderful cook, and you are quite pretty. Also, Henry Winslow has never recovered from something that happened almost a quarter of a century ago. There are two or three other little things too, but as you can see they don't help very much.'

'You'll solve it,' she said with quiet and

unshakable confidence. 'I thought you would that first time you came to the house.'

He was pleased at her faith in him, and if he'd chosen to confide in her he'd have agreed that he'd eventually identify her husband's killer, but that would have sounded too conceited to say aloud so he instead said, 'Well, once a crime is committed it can't be undone, so the police only have to persevere to eventually unravel it.'

He offered to help clear the table and do the dishes. She looked surprised, then embarrassed for some reason Lorillard did not quite fathom, and declined both offers, suggesting they go instead into the parlour, which is what they did.

There was an owl in one of the trees outside. It made its quick little mournful sound. Katie said either that owl or another one had been living in the tree for several years, and when he asked if it made her uneasy she shook her head.

'I like the sound. It's reassuring when I'm here alone at night.'

Lorillard had to admit the owl didn't

bother him in the least but he also had to admit to himself he would have expected a woman to feel differently.

She asked if he'd like a glass of port. He felt about wine essentially as he felt about tea, but because he thought she had perhaps bought the wine especially, he said he'd enjoy a glass. When she brought it, there were two glasses. He could tell by the way she sipped that she did not very often drink wine either.

Then she acted a little more relaxed as they talked, and the time passed very pleasantly, so perhaps the wine hadn't been such a bad idea after all.

She said candidly that she'd been trying to imagine how her husband's murderer had got into the house and how he'd made good his escape. Lorillard nodded, waiting for whatever had made her broach this topic. Everyone, even widows of murdered men, who were involved in crimes, became amateur sleuths, and Lorillard, unlike the vast majority of professional manhunters, had never scorned the advice nor been unwilling to listen to the theories, of these people.

She said, 'I told you I was polishing silver in the dining-room, Sergeant, and that the killer would have had to have gone up the entry-hall stairs which as you know are plainly visible from the dining-room. But after having some time to reflect upon that, I recall going into the kitchen twice, once for clean towels, another time for a moist sponge. The absences were no more than a minute or two each time, but it wouldn't take more than that for someone waiting in the shadows to hasten up the stairs, would it?'

Lorillard said he thought it probably wouldn't; he also said, 'Is there a second way to reach the stairs, aside from going through the kitchen and dining-room to the entry-hall?'

'Oh yes. If you wish I can show you. There is a small pantry between dining-room and kitchen. It has a side door leading to the entry-hall. He could have entered the house from out back, gone through the kitchen into that little pantry, then on through to the entry-hall.'

Lorillard nodded. 'Wouldn't that involve previous knowledge of the floorplan of the house?'

She nodded. 'That's what I've been driving at. As I said, I've had time to reflect, and it seems likely enough that this must be about how he got up there. But . . . '

'Yes?'

'Well, don't pistols make quite a bit of noise, Sergeant?'

Lorillard already had the answer to that. He had no proof, unless the lack of muzzleblast was in itself proof, but he was sure when all the facts were known it would be revealed that the murder weapon had been equipped with a silencer.

He explained how silencers worked, but he also had to say that fitting one to an automatic, as opposed to a revolver, posed some technical problems that only a proper gunsmith could overcome.

He already knew there was no gunsmith in Exeter. He'd determined that only a few weeks after going to work for the Exeter Police Department.

Katie, though, said something that surprised him. 'George does gunsmithing now and then, Sergeant. My brother used to hunt quite a bit. I remember him saying one time George Macklin repaired Edward's hunting rifle.'

Lorillard pondered this a moment, then finished his wine and made a private promise to go see Macklin in the morning. When he straightened around from putting aside the empty glass Katie was gazing at him.

She said, 'It couldn't possibly have been George, Sergeant.'

Lorillard dutifully nodded and arose. He told her it was late and he should be getting along. He also kept the topic from reverting to Macklin by thanking her warmly for the supper, for her delightful company, and for an evening he would never forget.

She got a little flustered at the door when he took one of her hands in both his big paws and squeezed. It was one of the few times he ever saw Katie get that way. She usually was so self-possessed, so matter-of-fact and steady.

In a way he liked her to look a little unsure of herself, and of him. He told her again how much he'd enjoyed himself, then made his exit, and because they were both New Englanders it never once crossed his mind to kiss her goodnight.

On the drive back to his room at the hotel he made a solemn resumé of all that had happened, and excluding the part touching upon George Macklin found it all very much to his liking.

7

Guns and Questions

Lorillard did not go directly to Macklin's car-shop the following morning. He went to visit Edward Arnold first, and not simply to verify what Katie had told him but also to see if, like everyone else, during the interim since Carlysle Stevens had been killed, Edward hadn't perhaps come up with something.

He hadn't. He was preoccupied with a warped roof when Lorillard arrived and came down the ladder saying that it looked like they might have an early autumn this year and he wanted to have a weatherproof topping on the old house in case, along with the freezing temperature, they might have early sleet, snow, or rain.

Edward was easy to talk to; he was considerate, diffident, at times voluble, at other times reticent. When Lorillard asked about hunting, Edward's blue eyes, steady and direct the same as Katie's, lingered upon Lorillard. He hadn't gone hunting in several years now, he said. The cold was beginning to get to him now that he was no longer a very young man. Furthermore, the game seemed to be retreating each year a little closer to the Canadian border, which was a goodly distance to travel.

Lorillard asked about guns. At once Edward's perplexed glance cleared. He took Lorillard inside the old house to a wall-rack where there was a rifle, a shotgun, and a holstered revolver. Edward gestured. 'That's all I own, Sergeant. Once, years ago, I had another rifle, but it was old and about half the time I had to have work done on it before I could go hunting, so I sold it.'

'What kind of work had to be done to it?'

'Well, one time both sights worked loose. Another time the breach got so loose it would foul the loads and spit back.'

'Who repaired it?'

'George Macklin. He doesn't do

gun-work any more, that I know of, and even in those days he wasn't really tooled up for it, but we were friends so he fixed the gun for me. Sort of a favour.'

'Is he a good gunsmith?'

Edward, obviously trying to guess what was behind each question, gave a cautious answer this time. 'Well, I got the impression he was just mechanically inclined, Sergeant, rather than very experienced. But the rifle worked all right when he'd finished with it.'

'Do you know of others he might have worked on guns for?'

'No.'

'You said you used to hunt, Edward; who else around Exeter hunts?'

Edward smiled. 'A few years back I'd have been able to name them one after another, but not any more. In those days when the season arrived they used to head out in droves. Brewster would close the hardware store, Dunston would declare a bank holiday, even Doc Bradford would load up a car and drive into the hills. But I doubt if any of that gang still hunts. Now it's the younger men or the out-of-towners.'

Lorillard let the talk drift a little, then he left Edward to his roof-repairing and drove round to George Macklin's place. George had Police Lieutenant Grady's patrol-car in his little shop for a tune-up and greeted Lorillard as though he'd half been expecting him. He pointed to a hot-plate where the coffee boiled and said he'd just had his morning pick-me-up, for Lorillard to help himself. Macklin appeared to be in a better mood than the last time Lorillard had called.

The coffee was strong and Lorillard took his cup over where Macklin was working, asked how the work was coming and when Macklin said he was booked ahead for a month Lorillard asked if he'd have time to do a little gun-smithing between cars.

Macklin looked up. 'I stopped working on guns three, four years ago, Mister Lorillard. There's no money in it in a place like Exeter and to do it right you need special tools.' Macklin leaned there gazing at Lorillard as though anticipating the next question or speculating on the reason for the first question.

Lorillard did not under-estimate his man; Macklin, for all his bluntness, was not dense. There would be no point now in asking leading questions so Lorillard said, 'How about pistols; have you worked on them?'

Macklin's lips pulled up slightly. He had expected this question. 'One or two, four or five years ago. One belonged to Josh Brewster at the hardware store, the other one belonged to a city policeman who is no longer in town.'

'Automatics, Mister Macklin?'

'No sir. They were both revolvers. I've never worked on an automatic.' The steady eyes turned knowing. 'I wish I could say I had though, and that it would help you find the man you're looking for.'

Lorillard thanked Macklin and departed. He hadn't been very hopeful, not after talking to Edward, so the disappointment wasn't deep nor lasting.

When he got back to his office Lieutenant Grady was waiting none too patiently. Grady was a gruff, rawboned, beefy man, scarred from brawls, with light blue eyes that were piercing and a burly, heavy-shouldered build. He followed Lorillard into the little private office saying he'd just been on a call over to the Bradford place.

'The doctor had a prowler last night.'

Lorillard was only indifferently interested. 'What was taken?' He felt obliged to ask it but felt very slight interest in the answer.

'Nothing, as far as Doc Bradford can determine. He drove out into the country to see a patient, he told me, and didn't realise he'd been burglarised until he got up this morning and found the back door had been pried open.'

Lorillard sat behind his desk eyeing Grady. 'Bradford may have frightened him off,' he said, referring to the burglar. 'Does he keep cash around the house; what would someone want of him?'

Grady lit a cigarette before answering. 'The usual stuff; jewellery, a little cash, maybe some antiques: The house is full of that old-time stuff. Been in the Bradford family for generations. But you never know about sneak-thieves.'

'Evidently nothing much was taken,' suggested Lorillard, 'or Bradford would have known it.'

'Yeah. That's what makes me think it was a prowler instead of a professional thief. But I thought you ought to know, him living next door to the Stevens' place.'

Lorillard thanked Grady and after the officer had left he telephoned Katie. She hadn't heard about the prowler, and in fact said she was very surprised to hear there had been one because, for some reason — she laughingly blamed it on the wine — she'd been unable to sleep the night before and had sat up reading until shortly before dawn, but had heard nothing next door and had seen nothing.

Lorillard doubted that the prowler had made much noise. He told Katie it might be a good idea to keep the windows and doors locked. He said he'd mention to Grady about having one of the patrol cars cruise Katie's area the following night.

By the time Lorillard finished talking to Katie it was noon and he was hungry. At the hotel dining-room, where he went because it was less likely to be crowded, he met Charles Dunston, and when he wished without much hope the banker wouldn't join him at his table, and took his seat, Dunston at once came over to ask if he might not sit at the same table. Lorillard agreed in his usual quiet way, which in this instance lacked enthusiasm because Lorillard lacked it, but Dunston didn't notice for as he sat, he said, 'Insurance adjuster was by the bank this morning, Sergeant. He asked some questions about Carlysle.'

Lorillard raised a polite eyebrow. 'What kind of questions?'

'Well, if the police had caught the murderer yet. Things like that. His company is reluctant to pay claims in murder cases. You realise they have to be very careful.'

Lorillard ordered, waited until Dunston had also given his order, then he said, 'Did he mention beneficiaries beyond Mrs. Stevens?'

'No. Just Katie. But there was a double-indemnity clause. The policy pays twice survivor's benefit in the event of violent death.'

Dunston kept looking at Lorillard after making that statement. Double-indemnity clauses weren't all that unusual, but on the other hand because premiums were so ruinously high, not many people carried that kind of insurance.

The banker said, 'Would old Carlysle, as tight-fisted as he was, pay for double-indemnity, Sergeant?'

Lorillard had no idea. 'You knew him better than I did, Mister Dunston. You tell me whether or not he would.'

Dunston started to shake his head, seemed to think better of it and said, 'You never know about people, do you? Maybe Carlysle thought something might happen to him. Otherwise, I'd be inclined to say he wouldn't pay what double-indemnity would cost. Then of course, as the adjuster said, it makes the affair look a little bleak from Katherine's standpoint.'

Lorillard let the waitress put a plate before him before answering. 'Usually those people go first to the police, Mister Dunston, and I haven't met this man yet.'

'He called at your office. He told me

Grady told him you were out. That was fairly early this morning.'

Lorillard had been out so he couldn't make much of a comment on this. 'He'll call back, then, I suppose,' he muttered, lifting his eating utensils. 'As for your implication concerning Mrs. Stevens . . .'

'No. Now you're putting words into my mouth, Sergeant. I didn't mean to imply Katherine was involved at all. It simply was one of the things the adjuster asked about — how she and Carlysle got along, things like that. And you'll have to admit double-indemnity makes a difference.'

Lorillard felt no urgency to admit any such thing. 'I'll be glad to see the adjuster,' he said, and fell to eating, which left Dunston across the table to talk on if he chose, or get down to the more practical matter of lunch.

They were on their dessert before Lorillard said, 'To your knowledge, Mister Dunston, does Doctor Bradford keep cash around his premises?'

Dunston looked up in surprise. 'Doc? I couldn't really say. Off the cuff, however, I can tell you between us he doesn't keep too large an account with the bank.'

'But his practice is profitable, isn't it?'

'I would most certainly think so. And living alone as he does the expenses can't be large.' Dunston chewed a moment then said, 'I think it's possible that he *does* keep cash around the house. It's a silly thing to do in this day and age. All banks are federally insured against loss. You can't say as much about all residences, can you?'

Lorillard didn't know. He didn't especially care, either.

'Is Doctor Bradford's credit good, Mister Dunston?'

The banker's answer was non-committal. 'He's never come round for a loan since I've been with the bank, and he doesn't buy much on tick that I know of. Then too, there is the medical association's loan fund. Doctors can get money through that outfit at bare-bones interest rates, you see, so actually Doctor Bradford doesn't especially need me. But I would imagine, if we were to run a financial check on him, Bradford would come out all right. Doctors do, you know.'

'I didn't know,' murmured Lorillard, and finished eating. 'Does he have any relatives that you know of?'

Dunston frowned slightly. 'A niece, I think, who lives at Fall River. Otherwise I don't believe he has any. He never married although I recall some of the tales I heard when he was away at medical school.'

'Gay blade?'

'Yes indeed.'

Lorillard smiled, counted out coins for his lunch and arose. 'It's been nice visiting with you,' he said, and left.

Charles Dunston, with an uneasy expression on his face, watched the big man's rolling exit. Dunston knew he'd just had his brain picked but he couldn't for the life of him imagine why. Surely Sergeant Lorillard couldn't suspect Doctor Bradford of murdering Carlysle Stevens. It was a ridiculous notion.

The trouble with a man like Lorillard was that no one ever knew what he might be thinking. Even his questions were somehow inserted into ordinary conversations until the person being interrogated did not realise he'd been questioned until later when he thought back to it.

Dunston did not particularly like Lorillard, but he was just now beginning to respect him, which, at least as far as Lorillard was concerned, was better anyway.

8

An Interloper

Phillip Carr, the insurance company's representative, was a youngish, pleasant, soft-spoken man whose personal attributes were perfect for his job. He made Lorillard feel as though he ought to take Carr under his wing and protect him from the evils of life.

He was round-faced, sometimes grave, sometimes smiling, and always polite. When Lorillard mentioned Carr's incursions round town, the younger man at once detected the annoyance and apologised for it before Lorillard had even commented.

He was, in a youthful way and most certainly without the finesse, the same kind of investigator Lorillard was. Perhaps by the time he was Lorillard's age he would also have that smooth polish.

But he proved himself a long way from

being Lorillard's equal now, because although the annoyance increasingly showed on Lorillard's face as the two of them talked in Lorillard's office, discussing Katherine Stevens, the widow, young Carr did not for a very long time realise he had irritated his companion.

He said it seemed probable to him, even though everyone he'd spoken to round Exeter, appeared to disagree, that Katherine Stevens most logically would benefit from, and have reason for participating in, the murder of her husband.

He also said his company would hold the claim in abeyance until it was quite satisfied, when all evidence was in, about just who had actually committed the murder, and who all was implicated in it. This, of course, was also another suggestion, couched in different language, saying about the same thing, and Lorillard's irritation made him offer a mild suggestion to Phillip Carr.

'Why don't you go back wherever you came from, Mister Carr, and just read the newspapers. When Carlysle Stevens's murderer is located it will be in the papers. That way you won't have to hang about in Exeter, just waiting.'

'Oh,' exclaimed Carr, 'I like the village. I don't mind hanging round at all. Moreover, my company expects me to make some attempt to help the police find the murderer. After all, Sergeant, there's quite a large sum of money involved. My company doesn't believe in giving its substance away.'

'I'm sure it doesn't. But the Exeter police don't need your assistance, Mister Carr, although they are grateful for your offer of assistance.'

'Sergeant,' stated the younger man, 'you have been on this case something like three weeks now. In our view — speaking for both myself and my company, you understand — in our view unless some positive steps are taken within ten days after a murder, each day thereafter the killer draws farther away from police detection.'

'Is that so,' said Lorillard. 'I find that very interesting, Mister Carr. May I ask who worked out that equation, you or the company?'

'Oh no. It's contained in a booklet written and distributed *gratis* to a select clientele by Doctor Benjamin Krack, the renowned horticulturist.'

'Horticulturist?'

'Yes. Flowers are his business, murder is his hobby. He's written a book on each subject. Then there's this little booklet. I hadn't considered it probable you hadn't seen it, Sergeant. I'll try and get you a copy. Some of the maxims seem almost classically applicable to the Stevens murder case. Drab widow, for example, who suddenly blossoms forth, handsome, sensual, cheery, where before her husband's death she was taciturn, mousy, a typical New England housewife.'

'You must be an authority on New England housewives, Mister Carr, to be so emphatic. You must also be very observant.'

'Well, now that you mention the latter, Sergeant, I must say I've made a particular practice of being observant. As to the former — well — wouldn't you say

Katherine Stevens has indeed changed — and right after the murder of her husband?'

Lorillard thought. Sensual? Katie Stevens sensual? He leaned back in his chair and stared a moment at the artistic pattern made by fly-specks upon the ceiling. She'd changed, of course, but then take anyone at all and run them through the same set of circumstances and they would also change. Lincoln demonstrated that with his Emancipation Proclamation. Carlysle Stevens's death had in effect been the same variety of emancipation from bondage.

'Sergeant?'

'I was just thinking, Mister Carr, how delightful it was to be your age, to have all those wonderful ideals and be dedicated to such lofty principles as arise from a union of horticulture and criminology.'

'But we were discussing Katherine Stevens, Suspect Number One in the murder of her husband.'

Lorillard rocked his chair forward,

fixed the younger man with a mild stare and said, 'She is *not* the prime suspect, Mister Carr. As for whatever steps may have been worked out prior to the expiration of ten days after Carlysle Stevens's passing, be assured his murderer is not getting farther and farther away.'

'Do you mean to say you know who the murderer is, Sergeant?'

'No, Mister Carr, if I'd meant that, I'd have said that.'

'But you have some idea, some clues pointing in particular to one person?'

'I'm afraid not.'

Phillip Carr looked disappointed and slightly betrayed. 'I was told round town that you were formerly of the Boston Police Department.' Carr said that as though his respect for the authorities of Boston was unbounded.

Lorillard smiled. 'It's true. But I'm not one of the brilliant sleuths. I simply hung in there until retirement age, then came to the country to keep my hand in without getting too much work piled upon me. Sorry to be such a disappointment.' Lorillard arose, picked up some papers off his desk and thoughtfully scowled at them.

Phillip Carr took his cue from that look of concentration and also arose. 'Well, it's been interesting,' he murmured. 'And of course we'll meet again.'

'If you stay in town I'm sure we will,' responded Lorillard with the softest kind of irony.

'Good day, Sergeant.'

Lorillard nodded, waited until the office door had closed behind Phillip Carr, then studied the papers in his hand more closely. Although he did not need a masculine corset, the price was very reasonable, the illustration was in colour, and who the hell put that brochure in his mail anyway?

He left the office shortly before noon and went for a long drive up-country. In fact before he got back to Exeter that night it was close to twelve o'clock.

There was a note from Lieutenant Gray in the hotel mailbox reporting that in his absence that afternoon a young man named Phillip Carr had lit a bonfire beneath the chair of Hamilton Brewster, old Joshua's brother, who was the oldest if not necessarily the best nor most successful lawyer in town.

Lorillard trooped upstairs to his room, flung aside hat, coat and tie, perched on the edge of a lumpy sofa and called the police station for Grady. Uniquely enough he got him. Grady usually did not remain on night-duty after being on day-duty.

When Lorillard asked about the note Grady said, 'Where were you all afternoon? Old Brewster called, mad as a hornet, then his brother called from the hardware store — you want to remember, Joshua is always a council man here in Exeter — and Mrs. Stevens called.'

'I drove up to Fall River.'

'Well, you picked a hell of a day to go joy-riding.'

Lorillard yawned. 'What specifically was Brewster upset about?'

'This Phillip Carr from the insurance company says his company may bring in a private investigator and its own team of attorneys. Ham Brewster wasn't too concerned about the big-city investigator, but it was like waving a red flag in front of a bull mentioning other, imported lawyers.'

Lorillard said, 'Okay, I'll look into it in the morning.' He would have rang off except that Grady wasn't quite ready to allow it just yet.

'You'd better get that insurance company to pull Carr out of here. He's also been circulating round town asking tons of questions.'

'I don't see that that does any harm. He's young, Grady, zealous, active, interested.'

'We got enough local amateurs with those same qualifications,' averred Grady. 'And besides, Carr's beginning to annoy people.'

Lorillard nodded over that. 'He seems to possess that ability, I'll admit, but I think we're near enough the end of the trail not to have to worry much about him.'

Grady read something into that in a flash. 'Hey,' he exclaimed. 'Have you got a good suspect?'

Lorillard, gazing mournfully at his wrist, said, 'Have you any idea what time it is? Goodnight, Grady.'

The chief of the uniformed police force was still speaking when Lorillard eased the telephone down, yawned again, and went to shower before bedding down. It had been an unusually warm day for springtime New England. In fact, even the night was warm. Lorillard speculated about this presaging a hot summer.

The following morning he'd scarcely got to the office before Joshua Brewster appeared with a complaint that actually was more in the nature of a lamentation.

'Who's he think he is, Sergeant, coming to our town threatening folks; my brother has been representing the old families of Exeter for forty years, and along comes this whippersnapper making threats. I tell you it's got to the point where this younger generation has got to be taught their place. I just can't imagine where the country is going, allowing riots in the streets, Democrats in the White House, and now young puppies like this Phillip Carr threatening people.'

'Where is your brother this morning, Joshua; why didn't he come to see me instead of sending you?'

'He had to go down to Boston for a couple of days on some litigation. But I promised to see you this morning for him. Now Sergeant I don't believe we have to put up with — '

'Joshua, Mister Carr is a free man in a free society. I spoke with him yesterday and although he impressed me as being eager, he didn't seem to be a man to make threats.'

Brewster's little bird-bright eyes quickened with hostility. 'Are you saying my brother made this up?'

'Of course not. But it's possible he misunderstood Mister Carr. In either case I'll get hold of Carr today and have a heart-to-heart talk with him.'

'Yes,' agreed Brewster, arising from the chair he'd preempted in Lorillard's little office. 'You do that. Tell him we handle things our own way hereabouts, and we will not tolerate outsiders coming here and telling us what to do.'

After Joshua Brewster had gone Lorillard telephoned Katie. She said it hadn't been anything important on her mind when she'd called him the day before, but her brother had come by to say the insurance company had sent a young man to town who had gone calling on Edward, and had seemed to disbelieve Katie wasn't somehow involved in Carlysle's passing.

Lorillard felt like cursing, instead he sighed and told Katie he'd drop round that evening to explain about Mister Carr, then he rang off, arose and left the office to do a little searching of his own.

He found Carr at Macklin's garage. It had been an elemental deduction; after all, Carr had seen Edward, Katie's attorney, Josh Brewster and just about everyone else the day before. It was probable he'd get round to George Macklin the next day.

Carr seemed mildly pleased when Lorillard walked up. George Macklin, looking less than enchanted, nodded at Lorillard then turned to drop down and slide beneath a car he'd been working upon.

Lorillard asked Carr if he'd turned up anything. The younger man had not, he said, but then he'd only been on the case a couple of days. Then he smiled. 'But I'll certainly tell you one thing, Sergeant Lorillard: Carlysle Stevens was not the most popular man in Exeter.'

Lorillard's response to that statement was mildly sardonic. 'You are just beginning your investigation, at that. Come outside the shop, please, Mister Carr.'

Out in the morning sunshine Lorillard finally let Phillip Carr have both barrels, and if those people including Katie could have heard Lorillard they would scarcely have believed their ears.

When he was finished Phillip Carr was pale, shaken, and properly contrite, and Lorillard had finished what he'd considered a necessary deviation from his normal vocation, which made it possible for him to get back to more important matters again. At least he *hoped* that might be the case, when he left Macklin's garage and got into his car for the drive back to the hotel for lunch, and afterwards, back to the office to co-ordinate a few things he'd been working on of late.

9

A Surprise at the Bank

Doctor Bradford saw Lorillard at his dining-table that night at the hotel as Bradford returned from caring for the same patient he'd looked in upon at their former similar meeting, and this time when Bradford joined Lorillard he ordered a full-course dinner, at the same time remarking to Lorillard that being a bachelor might indeed leave a man's life uncluttered and more or less uncomplicated, but it played hob with his digestive processes.

'People do better with regular meals, Sergeant, like regular habits. It may be less hectic on the nervous system being single and uninvolved, but only at the expense of the lower tract. Of course what that implies is that while bachelors, either lady or gentlemen bachelors, may protect one aspect of existence and health, they must seemingly only be successful at the expense of aggravating some other aspect. Pretty complicated isn't it?'

Lorillard agreed that it was indeed complicated. He also privately concluded it couldn't be either soluble or very important since people only lived just so long in any event. But what he said seemed to suggest he was interested.

'Carlysle Stevens, for example, Doctor Bradford, although I didn't know him, seems to me to have been the kind of person to have been influenced largely by his health.'

Bradford's pale eyes crinkled good-naturedly. 'Carlysle was as healthy as a horse. He didn't think so; the man always had some complaint — back ache, stiffening joints, mild indigestion, the usual hypochondriac symptoms, but that old devil would have lived to a hundred. His trouble was external, Sergeant, not internal.'

Lorillard raised a mild look to Bradford seeking an explanation. Bradford ate a moment before speaking again.

'Well, the darned old devil antagonised

people. Ask around, if you haven't already done so.' Doctor Bradford speared a slice of meat with his fork. 'His ailment had less to do with his physical condition than it had to do with his judgement. Patently, Sergeant, he made one too many enemies; picked on the wrong man and got himself done in.'

'You did the post mortem, Doctor. Was there anything that struck you as particularly strange?'

Braford chuckled. 'Massive brain damage, Sergeant. That's always strange when you encounter it. People Carlysle's age are supposed to die quietly in bed, not rush round getting themselves shot.'

'In attics,' murmured Lorillard.

'Yes of course, in attics.' Bradford ate, sipped tea, then said, 'And you, Sergeant, what have you turned up?'

'Very little, Doctor. Two bullets dug from the attic wall that failed to match the ballistics report on Stevens.'

Bradford put down his tea cup. 'Two bullets in the attic wall?'

Lorillard nodded, watching the surprise

spread across his companion's countenance. 'Yes. I suppose I should have explained. A man named Carlock killed himself a quarter century ago in the house behind the Stevens place. The slugs I found came from the gun he used.'

Bradford no longer acted amused or condescending. 'Ben Carlock,' he muttered. 'Of course. I remember the affair very well. But how in the devil did bullets from Carlock's gun get into the wall of Carlysle's attic workshop?'

'I can only guess, Doctor, but I think Carlock may have tested the weapon out a window.'

'Oh. Well, that would account for it at that, wouldn't it. But I'd never heard that before.'

Lorillard was sympathetic. 'I don't suppose very many people have heard about it, Doctor. Rather like the case of Carlysle Stevens — the bullets weren't where they should have been.'

'Eh?'

'Carlysle Stevens, Doctor. The two bullets that caused all the massive brain damage you mentioned a while ago, are nowhere in the attic wall, floor, or ceiling.'

Bradford pushed his meal away to lean upon the table. 'You've searched of course?'

'Every inch of the workshop. Yes indeed I've searched.'

'Well, but they *have* to be around there somewhere, Lorillard. After all you don't shoot a man in a —'

'Doctor, I've never said Carlysle Stevens was *shot* in his workshop. I've only said he was *found* there.'

They sat gazing at one another for five seconds before Harold Bradford leaned back to rummage his pockets for a cigar, which he lit carefully and afterwards held slightly to one side so the smoke wouldn't be offensive. Eventually he said, 'I don't understand, Sergeant. Are you now claiming Stevens wasn't killed in his workshop?'

'I never claimed that, Doctor. Not once. I had no reason to claim it after making a thorough examination of the attic, because right from the start there was reason to believe Carlysle Stevens hadn't been killed there. He was *lying* there, you know, very peaceably in fact, but that only establishes where the body was — it has no bearing in this case on where the man was actually killed.'

Bradford smoked and thought and eventually gave his head a slight wag of either doubt or amazement. 'Why in heaven would anyone carry Carlysle up all those infernal stairs and put him in the workshop, after killing him somewhere else?'

'If I were to guess, Doctor, I'd say the reason it was done that way was twofold: In the first place, the murderer did not plan to kill Stevens. It just happened. In the second place, since obviously if the body was found where Stevens had died it would have pointed a finger of suspicion at someone who had also been there — who was associated in the public mind with the place where the killing occurred — Stevens had to be got rid of. Why the murderer lugged Stevens up to his own workshop is anyone's guess; maybe he thought it would look better. Possibly that was the first thing that popped into his mind. Perhaps he even thought Katherine would then be accused. We'll have to wait for the murderer to answer that.'

Bradford smoked on, loose and slouched in his chair, his expression creased in concentration. 'I have to take it all back,' he ultimately averred. 'I've been of the opinion you weren't going to solve this thing.'

Lorillard smiled. 'Doctor, what I'm telling you is all preliminary and plain fact. I'm probably just as far from solving it now as I was the first time I saw that attic workshop.'

Bradford blew grey smoke at the ceiling, gazed round to find they were almost the only patrons still at dinner, then he said, 'And of course you've looked round for someone who thought they heard two gunshots.'

'No.'

'No? In a place like Exeter, Sergeant, gunshots are very rare. People would have heard them.'

'Not with a silencer on the weapon, Doctor Bradford.'

'Ahhh, and you know this to be a fact?'

'Hardly. Didn't you see a copy of the

ballistic report? It said there was very little burnt powder on the back of the head.'

'Yes indeed. In fact that was my own observation after performing the post mortem. My deduction was that Stevens had been shot from a goodly distance.'

'I think not, Doctor. My theory is that he was shot close up by someone he didn't expect to shoot him, who was using a gun equipped with a silencer. The ballistics report says the shooting occurred at close-range. If that is so, and there still were no powder-burns, then the gun was equipped with a silencer; something that would filter out the powder.'

Bradford sat staring at Lorillard and slowly drawing on his cigar for a moment longer, then he slapped his leg and reared back to shoot up out of the chair.

'By George, Sergeant, you are indeed a very observant detective. I'll never again believe you aren't a lot more shrewd and knowledgeable than you look and act. Well, it's getting late.'

After Doctor Bradford had departed

Lorillard paid for his dinner, went out onto the porch and fired up his pipe. He'd barely got comfortable when the desk-clerk came to say he was wanted on the telephone.

It was Charles Dunston at the bank, which was something of a surprise; Lorillard had always assumed that bankers went home in the afternoon, did not work through dinner-time.

'If you could spare a few minutes,' said Dunston, 'I'd like to see you here at my office at the bank.'

'Be right along,' said Lorillard, rang off and puffed on his pipe as he ambled back outside to the porch, where he hesitated a moment, then, deciding not to drive but to walk since the distance wasn't very great, hiked on down to the front sidewalk, turned left and paced along through the calm, starlighted night.

He'd had in mind a possible drive out to see Katie but that would not now be possible since it was already almost past a decent hour for paying calls, and whatever Charles Dunston wanted was certain to take another hour or so.

It was a fairly good surmise, for after Dunston admitted Lorillard and led him into the lighted privacy of Dunston's office, through a series of darkened offices, he said, 'Well, I suppose it was inevitable that something had to come up concerning Carlysle Stevens's estate, Sergeant, but I hardly expected it to be like this.'

Dunston handed Lorillard a piece of paper, then stepped behind his desk and sank down, remaining silent while Lorillard puffed his pipe and read. Afterwards, when the detective gazed calmly across at him, Dunston made a little fluttery gesture with both hands.

'I was surprised, to say the least. Also mystified.'

Lorillard leaned, knocked out the pipe, pocketed it and glanced again at the paper. It was an audit of the Stevens estate and it showed that Carlysle had withdrawn twenty-five thousand dollars, in cash, the day he was murdered. It also showed a similar withdrawal the day before, and the same amount withdrawn the day before that.

'Why?' asked Dunston, looking squarely at Lorillard. 'Seventy-five thousand dollars in three days, Sergeant. A man like Carlysle Stevens wouldn't have made any such withdrawals without the best of all reasons.'

Lorillard folded the paper, tucked it inside his coat and said, 'I doubt if anyone would have, Mister Dunston, and to hand you back the question, I'd like to hear your idea on why he'd do it.'

'But I have no idea, Sergeant. I came upon it late this afternoon — the first withdrawal that is — and kept my book-keeper overtime making a thorough and complete check.'

'Was it always the same teller who honoured the demands?'

'No. And that's something else. I talked to my tellers personally after this turned up. Stevens made each withdrawal from a different teller.'

'No explanations, no remarks?'

Dunston shook his head, looking slightly grim. 'Carlysle probably wouldn't have said much anyway. I can imagine how it must have pained him, making those withdrawals.'

'Any corresponding deposits among the other bank customers?'

'No. We checked that at once.'

Lorillard's brows gathered in a faint frown. 'And you have no ideas at all?'

'Sergeant, believe me, if I did have I'd tell you right this minute.'

Another time Lorillard might have been amused. Dunston was acting like a man who'd just witnessed a heinous crime, something perhaps akin to high treason or the striking of one's aged mother, or perhaps the robbing of a church. But he wasn't amused now, instead he was vastly puzzled.

He could see a glimmer of a connection between seventy-five thousand dollars and a bullet-riddled corpse — that was rather obvious — but he couldn't see Carlysle Stevens being so secretive, as though he were personally involved in something dishonest. He decided to go pay Katie that call after all, late as it was. He had no idea who else might have even a faint idea about what her husband had done.

But neither was he hopeful of learning much from Katie; Carlysle had never confided much in his wife.

Lorillard arose, thanked Dunston and allowed the banker to lead him back through the dark and gloomy bank to the front doors. There, when they parted, the banker said, 'I'll keep this in strictest confidence of course.'

Lorillard thought that would be best, thanked Dunston and left.

There was a sickle-moon overhead, hardly any traffic at all, and as Lorillard hiked back the way he'd come, to get his car, he noticed also that there was a little chilly breeze blowing in from the north.

10

Just Another Day

Katie was up reading a book when Lorillard arrived. She admitted him as though it were the most natural thing in the world for men to come calling late in the evening. She even put Lorillard in his favourite chair in the parlour then marched off to make him some coffee, without giving him any chance to protest.

He probably wouldn't have protested. He liked coffee, could drink inordinate amounts of it, and moreover he had something on his mind that did not permit much deviation, so he sat there in pleasant silence waiting for Katie to return, quietly pondering.

When the coffee came he launched into a quiet explanation of his reason for calling so late, mentioning the fact that Charles Dunston had called from the bank to the hotel when it was already past dinner time.

He then drew forth the paper he'd acquired at the bank and read off the dates of withdrawal and the amounts, appealing to Katie for enlightenment.

She looked perfectly round-eyed. Her initial response told Lorillard just about all he had to know. She said, 'Wherever did Carlysle get all that money?'

Lorillard put away the sheet of paper. If Katie hadn't known how much money her husband had, then she wouldn't be very likely to know what he'd been doing with it. Lorillard sighed. He'd always rather liked the masculine world of New England, but this was one time when it was not so amenable to his needs and wishes.

'I suppose he accumulated the money honestly,' he told Katie. 'What I'm interested in is why he withdrew it, what he did with it, and why he withdrew it a third each day instead of all at once.'

Katie, being very practical, said, 'Well, would the bank have that much money on hand, Sergeant?'

It was a perfectly reasonable question and perhaps a generation earlier the answer would have been in the negative. Not now; the Exeter Banking & Trust Company was liable to be called upon to have at least twice the amount withdrawn by patrons any one business day.

Lorillard said the cash would be there. He also said that aside from the inconvenience of carrying a great wad of cash that size in one's pocket, no normally prudent person would want that kind of money round the house, if for no other reason than because a fire or a burglary might destroy it.

'Did your husband act unnatural, Katie? Did he seem any different to you, in any way at all that you can recall, for the two days preceding his death, or the day he was killed?'

She shook her head, noticed Lorillard hadn't touched the coffee and said it would get cold. He lifted the cup, drank, put the cup down and said, 'How much of the time was he out of the house the day he died, or the two preceding days?'

She couldn't be too sure. She'd had her

own work to look after.

Lorillard felt like groaning. Instead he said, 'Katie, did he have any debts; had he mentioned paying anyone money or perhaps loaning them money?'

'Joshua Brewster,' she said. 'He did say something at supper the night before he died about having to go see Joshua Brewster at the hardware store the next day sometime. I don't remember the conversation but it seems to me, in looking back, it had something to do with money. But I can't recall whether it was a loan, a debt, or what it was.'

Lorillard relaxed slightly. 'He mentioned that the day before he was killed?'

She nodded, looking over at him. 'You can't possibly suspect Joshua Brewster, Sergeant.'

Of course he could, but he didn't argue with her. 'Seventy-five thousand dollars is an awful lot of money, Katie. I can assure you hundreds of people are killed every year for a good deal less. And this was in cash. Tell me; would your husband have withdrawn such a amount with equanimity?'

She came near to smiling. 'No, Sergeant, he would not have, no matter what the reason. Carlysle had very strongly-imbedded New England characteristics, and as you certainly must know touching one's principal is almost as bad as heresy. You may live off the interest but you never under any circumstances touch the principal.'

Lorillard smiled understanding. That's about the way he had her former husband sized up. It had disturbed him on the drive from the bank, not just having Stevens violate this cardinal tenet of New England life, but being up there in his attic workshop cheerily working with his wood-lathe afterwards as though he hadn't a thing on his mind.

It rang false from start to finish.

He arose saying he'd see Brewster at the hardware store first thing in the morning, then let her lead him to the front door and out upon the yonder porch where weak moonlight made no impression upon the great tree-shadows down across the yard.

There were lights among the houses

across the road and elsewhere, next door for example at the Bradford place, and on the other side as well.

That little chill remained, too; putting one in mind of the fact that springtime hadn't yet decided to yield to summer. Katie gazed at the stars, at the soft-lighted treetops, and said, 'Sergeant, what possible use could my husband have for seventy-five thousand dollars?'

She didn't qualify the statement, which would have made it easier to answer; she simply made her remark as though that much money were almost ridiculous by itself. Lorillard could come close to agreeing that it was ridiculous. Objectively, a person couldn't go about with seventy-five thousand cash dollars in a pocket, and if he lived as abstemiously as old Carlysle had insisted upon living, then there was no point in even owing that much money.

But Carlysle *had* withdrawn it, and in cash, so the riddle was only deepened by this kind of speculation. Moreover, it was Lorillard's job to determine why the money had been taken out of the bank, and what had been done with it, so seventy-five thousand dollars was actually not ridiculous at all. Not when it had somehow to be connected with murder.

'The inconsistencies,' he mused aloud to her as though she were his confidant, 'are troublesome, Katie. I think I have a composite image of your husband, and while it differs in some respects from the general image around town, still, with respect to finances I'll have to accept the general opinion.'

She smiled at him, her eyes full of trust, and when he bade her good-night she said he was not to worry, that whatever was behind all this he most certainly would discover.

On the drive back to the hotel, after eleven o'clock with the town slumbering on all sides, he hoped he wouldn't have to disappoint her. He also marvelled that a woman could be so serenely indifferent to finances, although he had as a matter of fact encountered other women whose interests were just about as fiscally irresponsible.

He retired that night with a fist-sized

knot weightily settled in the middle of his mind. It kept him awake for perhaps an hour, and when he awakened the following morning it was still there, nagging him through his ablutions, his breakfast, and the drive to the office where he telephoned Charles Dunston to see if anything had turned up at the bank.

Nothing had, according to Dunston, despite the banker's resumé of yesterday's revelations, but Dunston also said he wasn't finished making his quiet investigation yet and would call back if anything turned up.

Lorillard had his daily course fairly well plotted. The first step was to call Boston, to contact the office of the Federal Bank Examiner, explain who he was and what he wanted. The gentleman he spoke to, named Harrington, was not perturbed by Lorillard's identity nor his request, and when Lorillard offered a mild apology for calling Harrington said, 'Not at all, Sergeant. We get at least one of these tracers every day. You must realise, though, that while our endeavour is essentially a monitoring one, we can't reach out and put our finger on who deposits what within a matter of hours. It may take several days, but rest assured I'll personally take charge of this and call you back the moment there's anything to report.'

Lorillard was putting the telephone aside when Lieutenant Grady entered and said Phillip Carr the insurance adjuster had just parked his car out front. Grady was slyly smiling. 'You'd better duck out the back door,' he advised Lorillard, then withdrew from the room.

When Carr came along a few moments later Lorillard was standing by his office window, hands behind his back, studying a weakening long shadow made by a brick corner of the building. Lorillard turned and nodded, then motioned his caller to a chair although Lorillard made no move to leave his standing position back by the window.

'You're out bright and early,' he told the younger man.

Carr studied Lorillard's thick, massive bulk with an expression of suppressed disillusionment. 'I've finished making the rounds,' he said. 'Excepting Macklin and the banker everyone was co-operative.'

Lorillard smiled; George Macklin was civil at his best, surly at his worst, and by temperament was not likely to be co-operative even with someone he knew, but with someone he considered a rank outsider, he would, like most other New Englanders, show a distinctly brusque and indifferent attitude.

Lorillard said, 'When did you see the banker?'

Carr glanced at his watch. 'Half an hour ago. He said he was too busy to talk to me; that perhaps later in the day he'd have the time. It was quite a switch from the way he acted when I first saw him day before yesterday. In fact he was one of the first — we always make a point of seeing the bankers first, you know; they have a way of knowing a good deal about people.'

Lorillard continued to smile as he went back to the desk, hauled out his chair and sank down. 'What are your plans now, Mister Carr?'

'Well, I thought you might have something to tell me.'

Lorillard's mild gaze lifted. 'I? For example.'

'I saw you talking to the doctor last night at the hotel dining-room. It seemed a rather animated conversation.' Carr showed no signs of embarrassment as he admitted casual spying.

Lorillard made no point of this, he simply said, 'You have talked to Bradford. You could go talk to him again this morning. In any event, we didn't make any great discoveries last night. He seemed surprised when I told him I'd found two old bullets embedded in the murder-room of the Stevens' house, and he also seemed surprised that I didn't believe Stevens was murdered in the room, but had been killed elsewhere and had been carried to that room and dumped on the floor.'

Lorillard knew before he said these things that Carr would not know them, although in a metropolitan police establishment Lorillard would probably have been obliged to keep a current report available for just such purposes as Carr represented, in Exeter no such regulations existed, therefore Carr sat and stared and said nothing until Lorillard had finished speaking. Then he got a pained, almost indignant expression on his face.

'All of this is vitally important to my company,' he said a trifle stiffly.

Lorillard could have agreed with that since it was obviously the truth. On the other hand, as he explained, he was a lone detective, without secretarial help, and his primary interest was not so much in making reports for filing as he was in locating a murderer.

Carr may, or may not, have accepted that excuse. He said, 'I've read the Coroner's report, as well as a number of editorials in back-issues of that asinine little local daily newspaper. There was no mention of Stevens having been killed elsewhere.'

'The Coroner, Mister Carr, is not an investigative individual. As for the editor and the daily paper — you've seen it, have read it. I shouldn't have to say more. As for the rest — don't fret Mister Carr.'

The younger man's expression underwent a slow change. 'I think I made a bad judgement in your case, Sergeant Lorillard.'

'You won't have been the first.' Lorillard looked at his wrist. 'I've got to go see a man, so I hope you'll excuse me.'

After ridding himself of Carr, Sergeant Lorillard strolled forth to find Grady, who was in the small cell-block out back feeding lye-like black coffee to a groaning man in one of the cells who had been picked up the night before hopelessly drunk. The man happened to be the local church sexton which was not an altogether incompatible situation although not everyone in town would concur with that.

Grady greeted Lorillard with a wry grin. 'You'll meet everyone back here if you hang round along enough,' he said, and left the bad-off inmate with his big tin cup of coffee to walk back a little distance, out of earshot of the prisoner, with Lorillard.

'Tell me something about Charles Dunston,' said Lorillard. 'Has he ever been in trouble?'

Grady, who should perhaps have been shocked, was not; police work even in villages induces cynicism. 'Not that I ever heard of. Certainly not since I've been on the force.'

'Have you ever heard rumours that might reflect upon his management of the bank?'

Grady shook his head. 'No. In fact, even among the people who don't like the banker, and he has 'em just like all the rest of us, I've never heard a breath of scandal about how he runs the bank.'

Lorillard said, 'Thanks,' smiled at Grady and strolled back up through the building to the front foyer, and on out into the morning sunshine, leaving Grady standing back there scratching his head and looking quizzical. It wasn't much, but every cent of Grady's savings were in Dunston's bank; if there was any funny business going on Grady wanted to know about it. He promised himself to look Lorillard up later in the day and get some straight answers.

His recuperating drunk groaned loudly and Grady turned back towards that particular cell again.

11

An Unexpected Bit of Violence

Joshua Brewster, surveying Lorillard from behind his glasses with that bird-like brightness, bobbed his head over the request to speak privately and took Lorillard to his little cluttered and dingy back-office. Lorillard seemed oversize for that room even when he sat, which at least took his head from a near brush with the ceiling.

'I'm interested in whatever you can tell me,' he told Brewster, 'of Carlysle Stevens's business dealings.'

Brewster bobbed his head, removed his glasses and proceeded to polish them briskly on a clean handkerchief. 'From time to time 'Lysle and I co-operated in things.'

'For example, if you don't mind, Mister Brewster.'

'Well; before the highway came

through — the new one, that is — 'Lysle and I discovered the route to be followed and bought some land on both sides of the right-of-way.'

'I see. Then sold it at a profit.'

'Yes.'

'Anything else?'

Brewster replaced the glasses, squinted through them a moment and gently smiled. 'We acted on some inside tips my cousin down in New York gave me, Sergeant; stock market tips. We made a little money speculating like that now and again.'

'Any big money involved in any of these transactions, Mister Brewster?'

The merchant pursed his lips and ceased to smile. His eyes fiercely probed. 'I'd like to know what this is all about, Sergeant.'

Lorillard ignored the question. 'What did Stevens come to see you about the day he died?'

Brewster blinked rapidly several times and forgot he hadn't got an answer to his question. 'He didn't come to see me that day, Sergeant. I hadn't seen 'Lysle

Stevens for several days, perhaps a week, before he was killed.'

'He told his wife he had to see you the day he was killed, Mister Brewster.'

Now, the merchant began to fidget on his chair. Lorillard's great bulk and rock-steady stare did nothing to alleviate his increasing distress. 'I can't help what he told Katherine, Carlysle Stevens did not step foot in my store that day. Nor for several days before, in fact.'

Lorillard was convinced. He then said, 'What would Stevens be doing carrying around seventy-five thousand dollars in cash?'

That staggered Brewster, his eyes shot wide open. 'Goodness gracious; seventy-five thousand dollars. And in cash?' He stared at Lorillard as though the detective had said something obscene. 'Did he have that much money with him the day he died?'

Again, Lorillard turned the question away. 'Did he have anything pending with you, Mister Brewster; stock deals, land deals, anything that would require considerable cash?'

'No. We never handled cash. And we never got that involved either. Seventy-five thousand dollars, Sergeant, would have purchased the entire block of buildings where my store sits. We never even discussed anything that large. Nor would I have participated in anything involving such sums of money.'

Lorillard got to his feet. He perhaps should have felt disappointment, but he didn't for a very good reason. At long last he had his teeth into something — the missing wealth. He had to find it, find out what was done with it, and after that there would in all probability be a murderer in the background. He thanked old Brewster and left the store. Brewster, exactly as Grady had done at the police station, stood like a man thunderstruck watching Lorillard depart.

It was a short drive to the bank but finding a place to leave the car took half again as much time. Afterwards, finding the bank busy, Lorillard was about to depart when Dunston came out looking a little smug.

'I think we're on the trail,' he said,

drawing Lorillard towards a corner like a conspirator. 'George Macklin came in yesterday and deposited twelve thousand dollars in cash.'

It struck Lorillard as odd but not terribly odd. People normally did not transact business in cash. Still, Macklin was not an average person. What stuck hardest in Lorillard's mind though, was something else. He mentioned it quietly.

'If it was part of the Stevens money why would Macklin wait this long before depositing it?'

Dunston wagged a sly finger. 'Isn't that what any smart person would do, Sergeant? After all, if he'd waltzed in here the day after . . . Do you follow me?'

Lorillard got the implication, but it didn't phase him. Talking to Dunston, though, wasn't going to help much, so he escaped as soon as he could, buying his escape with a promise to telephone Dunston later if he learned anything.

He drove directly to the Macklin place, and found both George Macklin and Edward Arnold sitting at a workbench in the cluttered workshop having a chat over bottles of coke. When Lorillard filled the doorway both men looked up. Arnold's reaction was predictable: he smiled. Macklin's face was stonily impassive until Lorillard walked on up, then Macklin scowled. Evidently this was one of his surly days.

'Coffee-break?' asked Lorillard cheerfully.

Arnold nodded, still amiably smiling, but Macklin said, 'Why the hell are you always harassing people, Sergeant? You aren't going to find a murderer hiding here in my shop.'

'No harassment intended,' murmured Lorillard, gauging the other large man's mood and bracing for additional unpleasantness. 'I have a job to do just like everyone else. This morning it includes talking privately to you, if you don't mind.'

'And if I do mind?' growled Macklin, hunching thick shoulders forward where he sat.

Lorillard waited a moment, then said, 'We'll still talk.'

Macklin sat studying Lorillard. Edward

Arnold got up, took his three-quarters-full bottle of cola and stepped away. 'I'll be out back,' he said to Macklin. 'You two'll want to be alone.' He nodded quickly at Lorillard and fled out through a rear door.

Macklin's colour mounted. Lorillard had heard tales of the man's unpredictable and yeasty disposition but this was the first time he'd ever encountered Macklin's overt wrath. Trying to head it off he took the seat Arnold had vacated and said, 'Look, George, this is a lot more difficult for me than it is for you. All I want is an answer to one question.'

'Well, you'll play hell getting it, comin' in here and running people off. Lorillard, for a plugged cent I'd throw you out.'

Lorillard sighed, studied Macklin a moment, then arose with quiet resignation, stepped back one step and nodded his head. 'Do it,' he said. 'Throw me out.'

Macklin's eyes blanked out, his lips flattened, the powerful shoulders moved as Macklin slowly pushed himself up from the table. 'All right,' he said softly, and started round the bench.

'You asked for it, Lorillard.'

Macklin, the former-logger, was a scarred, burly, large and powerful man. When he got clear of the table and raised heavy arms, Lorillard made his move. He stepped in, cracked Macklin over the bridge of the nose, turned his head with another blow to the temple, then moved sideways and backwards and dropped both arms.

Macklin was surprised and his eyes ran water. He swore and jumped. Lorillard wasn't there when the big fists slashed air. Macklin checked his rush, spun and started back again. That time Lorillard did not give an inch. Macklin fired a left that connected but the cocked-right struck Lorillard's upraised forearm and rode it up harmlessly overhead; at the same time Lorillard blasted a sledgehammer blow into Macklin's unprotected middle, caught him as he started to bend with a strike on the shoulder that half spun Macklin, then he caught the other big man, whirled him and heaved him bodily over the bench. It crashed over with

Macklin, breaking two of the wooden legs.

Macklin lay amid the wreckage while Lorillard picked up a clean cloth off a nearby toolbox and proceeded to wipe his hands. Macklin's shirt had had grease on it.

Edward Arnold, standing in the rear doorway, looked aghast. George Macklin, breathing hard and blinking away tears from his injured nose, muttered something fierce under his breath and rolled up onto his uninjured side to study Lorillard.

He grinned.

Lorillard grinned back. 'Sometimes it helps a man's disposition, getting the meanness out of it.' He bent to extend a hand for Macklin to use in getting back to his feet. Macklin had a little difficulty breathing so he picked up a stool, set it to rights and gingerly eased down.

'You pack quite a wallop,' he said. 'Okay, Sergeant, what was that question you wanted to ask me?'

'Where did that twelve thousand dollars come from you put in the bank yesterday, George?'

Macklin was gingerly exploring his ribs when he answered. 'I sold some acreage on the outskirts of town a couple of miles from here. The buyers were a pair of strangers from New York. I wouldn't take their damned cheque so they went and cashed it and brought me the cash.' Macklin shifted his attention to the bridge of his nose, which was turning a fine shade of purple. 'Call Charles Dunston at the bank, he ought to know if anyone cashed a cheque that size at his bank yesterday or the day before.'

Lorillard went to the Coca-Cola machine, put in a coin, got his chilled drink and took it back towards the centre of the room. Damn Dunston anyway. He drank, considered the broken bench and said he'd pay the damages resulting from their little exchange.

Macklin grinned and shook his head. 'It was worth it to find out you aren't just the big ox I thought you were. Anything else I can do for you?'

There wasn't, so Lorillard finished his drink and left. He was angry all the way back to his office. He considered stopping off at the bank but in his present frame of mind didn't believe that would be wise.

Later, cooled off considerably, he telephoned Dunston and asked if a twelve thousand dollar cheque had been cashed, and while he held the telephone waiting for Dunston to check on that, he stuffed and lit his pipe. It was only early afternoon but after the brisk exercise at Macklin's garage he felt he was justified in a little pre-supper relaxation.

Dunston reported, somewhat sheepishly, that a cheque for that amount of money had been cashed. He offered a reasonable excuse for what had happened; he did not see the lists of cashed cheques each day, unless there was some kind of irregularity, and there hadn't been.

Lorillard let several seconds go by in strong silence before he coldly but politely thanked Dunston and rang off.

The banker would understand Lorillard's reaction and his mood, which was all Lorillard had wanted. Afterwards he leaned back, puffed on the pipe, and softly smiled to himself.

It had been an interesting excursion, that trip out to Macklin's garage. He'd always heard that loggers considered themselves very tough and capable. Policemen, particularly from tough large cities, thought of themselves in pretty much the same way.

It had been enlightening to discover that loggers, as represented by big, rugged and surly George Macklin, might be handy in brawls with other bear-like oafs, but in a class with a variety of men who had to learn quite early in their profession to cope with all manner of troublemakers, loggers weren't in the same league with policemen.

Not even greying policemen.

Lorillard's ego was boosted immeasurably by this revelation. He wasn't all that over the hill yet, after all.

Grady came round an hour before quitting time to ask if Lorillard really thought the bank was shaky. Lorillard assured him he'd never meant to imply any such thing; that as far as he was concerned the Exeter Banking & Trust

Company was as sound as the U.S. Mint. Perhaps, all things considered, even sounder.

Then Lorillard went home to the hotel for an early dinner. He had to acknowledge one thing; he wasn't in the best of shape. That scuffle had made him feel a little tired.

12

Lorillard Reflects

If Edward Arnold hadn't witnessed the altercation in Macklin's garage it might have been relatively easy for big George Macklin to conceal what had actually happened from almost everyone, but there was one person he couldn't have fooled, and that was Doctor Bradford to whom he had to go for a patch over the injured bridge of his nose.

Bradford, a shrewd and knowledgeable practitioner, said nothing until he'd also examined the bruised ribs, then he said, 'Well, George, if you insist on going about with a chip on your shoulder you ought to make it a point to antagonise only smaller men. Whoever he was, take my word for it he could hit like a kicking mule. It's a wonder your nose isn't smashed flat, and those ribs aren't broken. Who was he?'

'Sergeant Lorillard.'

Bradford stopped the examination, reared back and stared. 'Lorillard, the detective?'

'Doc,' said Macklin, 'don't let that shuffling gait or that gentle smile fool you. He knocked me around like I was some damn fool of a schoolboy.'

'Who started it, George?'

'Will you just fix the nose, Doc?'

'I see. So you started it. All right, I'll fix the nose, and I'll also charge you ten dollars too, since you had to try someone and got the worst of it.' Bradford worked a few moments then began gently shaking his head from side to side as though he could hardly believe Lorillard had done all that damage to notoriously rugged and tough George Macklin.

Edward Arnold told his sister over the telephone. She was shocked. He also told Henry Winslow whom he found in the hardware store talking to Joshua Brewster. They were also shocked, but it was a different variety of shock from that Katie had felt.

Before quitting time that same evening Lieutenant Grady had also heard the details, not much enhanced by the time they got to him, and went along to Lorillard's office to check on them for veracity.

Lorillard was lolling behind his desk smoking. He said that had to be about the way things happened because although he, himself, had been too occupied at the time to take notes, the beginning and ending were authentic.

Then Lorillard left, leaving Lieutenant Grady chortling because he'd had a run-in or two with George Macklin and there was no affection felt between them.

Lorillard had bathed and changed and was coming down into the hotel lobby a little shy of six o'clock when he encountered Harold Bradford. The doctor clapped Lorillard on the shoulder.

'Cracked the bridge of his nose, dented a couple of ribs, and gave his ego its most grievous blow, Sergeant, but all in all I think you've earned his respect and made a friend. Macklin's one of those neolithic throwback-types; believes in the simple virtues — and force. He got a pretty good shellacking today, so from now on you'll be welcome at his garage.'

Bradford trooped on up the stairs, little black bag in hand. Lorillard turned to watch a moment, then went on out across the foyer to the dining-room to his usual table. He had a hunch the medical practitioner would come join him at supper after a bit.

He was right, and this being the third such intrusion Bradford unceremoniously dumped his bag upon the seat of an unoccupied chair, signalled the waitress, sank down with an unsteady sigh and said, 'It's O'Leary on the second floor. He's coming loose in the vitals. Would you believe he was in the Spanish-American War? If you recall, that was in 1898.'

Lorillard was patient with this run of casual talk but when his meal arrived he went to work over it as though Doctor Bradford were not there.

'He doesn't know how old he is,' went on Bradford, judiciously eyeing the size of Lorillard's steak and the mound of starchy potatoes. 'By my estimate, since he had to be at least sixteen years old, and had to look still older, to enlist in the army, and that splendid little war was fought something like seventy years ago, O'Leary has to be at least eighty-six, and more than likely he's ninety years old.'

Lorillard nodded. 'He's entitled to start falling apart, then.'

Bradford agreed, let the waitress serve him, then acted as though he weren't particularly hungry after all. He drank a cup of tea, watched Lorillard stolidly tucking away his meal, and wryly smiled. 'I envy you your appetite, Sergeant. I'll wager you sleep like a baby too, eh?'

Lorillard smiled slightly. 'Clear conscience, Doctor. A little money in the bank, a pension coming in each month, and very little actual ambition. Dumb but content. And you're right, I usually do sleep like a baby.'

'Even though the Stevens matter still isn't resolved?'

'I'm hired to do my best, Doctor, not work miracles.'

'But you are confident, aren't you?'

'About the Stevens murder? I think I'd

just say that I'm hopeful.'

'Anything new?'

Lorillard ate a moment then put aside his knife and fork to reach for the coffee. 'No, nothing new. But there seem to be plenty of diversions. For instance, today I learned Macklin deposited twelve thousand dollars at the bank, in cash.'

Bradford looked mildly surprised. 'He didn't mention it to me when I was patching him up. Does it have a bearing?'

'No. He sold some land. But that's what I mean about diversions. Everyone is very helpful. So helpful in fact I've been hopping around like a cat on a hot tin roof.'

Bradford grinned. 'Would you like another diversion? Actually, it's only a theory. You won't have to check it out.'

'Shoot,' said Lorillard, finished with everything except the coffee.

'Stevens was approached by someone for a loan. He puts out money at high interest now and then, you know. This time he refused.'

'I see. And the person seeking the loan

flew into a frenzy and shot him. One question, Doctor: Do people going out to beseech loaners for money usually carry loaded automatics?'

Bradford chewed thoughtfully, then said, 'Well, that's a good question and I hadn't considered it. But isn't it possible that this person, knowing Stevens perhaps and fearing a refusal, might in his desperation have made up his mind to rob the old devil if he were turned down?'

'It's possible, yes. And where would they have met?'

'At the Stevens' place, of course.'

'But Stevens wasn't killed at his residence, Doctor.'

'Oh, yes. I'd forgot. Well, they met by pre-arrangement somewhere else, then.'

'Perhaps Brewster's hardware store? That's where Stevens told his wife he was going the day he was killed.'

Bradford raised his eyes, studied Lorillard's calmly impassive features a moment then said, 'That's something else I hadn't heard. You know, Sergeant, I believe I'm beginning to respect you also. It's just possible Macklin's not the only one who's been under-estimating you all along.'

Lorillard fished out the money for his dinner, placed a few extra coins beside his plate for the waitress, and felt through his pockets for the pipe and pouch. After he'd lit up, making no attempt to leave the table as was his usual custom, he said, 'Doctor, your theory is reasonable, and since Stevens was not too well-liked, I suppose you'd say his murderer was probably someone local. Someone, say, who had reason to dislike Stevens.'

Bradford nodded and continued to eat. 'Otherwise,' he mumbled, 'he wouldn't have been carrying the gun, Sergeant.'

'The gun with the silencer on it, Doctor. But that's a stickler because people in small towns don't usually own silencers, and that leads us to the possibility that your theoretical suspect *knew in advance* he was going to kill someone; he may even have been planning the Stevens killing a long while — loan request aside. In fact, he may not even have wanted the loan at all; he may just have wanted to kill Stevens.'

Bradford was listening closely now, so when Lorillard finished speaking the doctor said, 'Why? Why would he want to kill Stevens? I should imagine George Macklin, his disposition being what it is, or perhaps Katherine Stevens who had to put up with Carlysle all these years, would be prime suspects, but aside from those two, why would someone else want to kill Stevens? Of course he wasn't popular, and all that, but there has to be emotional commitment before someone commits murder. At least in the psychiatric context I'd be inclined to say there had to be emotional involvement.'

Lorillard was agreeable. 'I think that is very true, Doctor, but I'd have to defer to your knowledge on the subject to prove it. As for your question of who, beside Katherine and Macklin, I'd say it could be anyone at all. Stevens has lived in this town all his life, he knew everyone and everyone knew him. His business dealings have affected a number of people. His personality has doubtless rubbed people the wrong way and his character hardly qualified him for the title of the most lovable resident. So when you say who beside his widow and George Macklin could possibly be sufficiently involved to kill him, I'd say — anyone who's lived in Exeter any great length of time.' Lorillard removed the pipe, peered into its fragrant bowl, tapped a little ash into the tray near at hand and smiled disarmingly at Doctor Bradford. 'There are people who persist in believing it was a burglar caught in the act who did the killing, but of course they don't know enough of the facts to say otherwise.'

Bradford nodded, leaned back in the chair and tried to match Lorillard's smile. 'I have a feeling, Sergeant, that you are only taking your time about making an arrest. My impression is of a cat crouching near the unsuspecting mouse.'

Lorillard shook his head and arose from the table. 'You've 'way over-estimated me, Doctor. I have a few facts, but actually they don't help as much as they tantalise.'

'But you've narrowed the field considerably.'

Lorillard's eyes twinkled ironically.

'From the entire state of Massachusetts, Doctor, to just one entire village.'

They parted on that little note of jocularity, Lorillard strolling out to the porch for a bit, Doctor Bradford heading homeward through a chilly but clear and handsome night.

Later, Lorillard also retired, and upstairs in his room with starshine touching down upon all the peaceful roof-tops of Exeter, he stood a moment by his window looking outward, his mood one of sardonic affection for this unspoilt bit of New England with its sturdy stock and its Puritan virtues, where a murderer lurked amid all the propriety, all the traditional ethics, all the respect for law and order that mark oldtime New England's descendants.

It didn't lessen his feeling for the people any; in fact the reason for his affection was the exact fact of this aberration. Conformity was perhaps desirable in Exeter, as it was elsewhere in order that people living together in social proximity might get along, but there was a rogue loose in Exeter, and that saved the place from being another little stuffy, dull place.

He was sure he knew who the rogue was.

It was late, he'd had a long day, there was no reason to believe the following day wouldn't be just as arduous, so Lorillard retired, and that which so often is the case with thoughtful people, occurred: He couldn't go to sleep.

For an hour and a half he lay there, thick arms beneath his head, gazing at the little square patch of sky visible beyond his street-side window, no particular thought holding his attention but a number of interlocking ones coming and going.

When he finally slept he did not know, but when he awakened it was with a keen and healthy hunger and the inhabited dark sky was now softly pale and starless.

He had it in mind driving out to see Katie this morning so he dressed slowly and with some care, which was not the usual thing for Lorillard. Also, he had in mind going to the local representative of the Commonwealth Attorney to see about getting a murder warrant, and it would look better if he weren't attired like someone who'd gone camping and had used his clothing for his tent.

It helped, also, that the day was mildly overcast, at least in the morning, so the heat was minimised by the time Lorillard finished breakfast and walked out of the hotel to his car.

In fact, he had a feeling that this just might be a very interesting day all round. About things of this nature he frequently was quite correct.

13

Giving Substance to a Ghost

Katie was pleased to see Lorillard. She was briskly polishing the dining-room table with lemon-oil when he arrived, and because the great old oaken table was large, the exertion of shining it stimulating, Katie's cheeks were flushed, her eyes bright, her breathing deep, when she went to the door to admit Lorillard.

And she blushed, making her colouring more pronounced, as she explained the reason for her gloves, apron, and the very noticeable, but pleasant, scent of lemons in the house.

She took Lorillard to the parlour, as she invariably did, and then said she'd get him some coffee. He declined with thanks on the grounds that he had only very recently had breakfast, then he had to answer her question about the unpleasantness with George Macklin before he could get down to what had brought him.

She nodded as he gave her an accounting of the Macklin matter, neither surprised nor very disapproving, then she admitted that George was like that, had been ever since his wife had passed on, and in fact even before that, although in those earlier days his surliness was much less pronounced.

'I used to get so exasperated with him,' she said. 'Carlysle would try to talk to him and they'd end up on a sour note every time.'

'Macklin's fault every time?' asked Lorillard mildly, making Katie look at him for a moment before answering.

'No, but they certainly had that in common — flinty New England dispositions.' She smiled. 'My personal feelings for the past year or so have inclined me to feel that if George Macklin and Henry Winslow would stop moping about and find new loves and wives, they'd both be a lot better off than living like a pair of recluses.'

'Katie,' said Lorillard. 'Why is it that everyone speaks of your late husband without affection?'

She looked at Lorillard, then slowly removed the gloves she wore when doing the heavy house cleaning and smiled. 'Sergeant Lorillard, if you were not a New Englander yourself, I don't suppose an explanation would sound very reasonable.' She raised her eyes to his face. 'I have wondered all my life, Sergeant, why New Englanders find it so difficult to display affection. Even among lovers it isn't the same in New England. But for me to speak with affection of other men — that's unheard of, isn't it?'

Lorillard nodded and settled back in his chair. He knew she would have more to say just from watching her. He was right.

'Well. Of course my husband was stingy and grumpy and abstemious. And he was also harshly outspoken at times. But it's habit among New Englanders to esteem someone like that; they work at being that way, too, don't they?'

Again Lorillard nodded.

'I suppose the hypocrisy is that the majority of them aren't that way at all.

Isn't that what you're digging for, Sergeant?'

He met her gentle smile with a twinkle. 'Something like that, Mrs. Stevens. I've been a long while trying to flesh out an image for your husband, and invariably I ran into one inconsistency: The man's actions as opposed to his reputation.'

Katie said, 'But, Sergeant, you surely know what the most cherished of all New England reputations involves? First, you must be taciturn, unsmiling, as flinty as the stony fields themselves. Then you must have a capacity for making money. Finally, you must earn the right to be considered miserly, disagreeable, but moderately well-off.'

Lorillard chuckled. She had described the reputation most cherished by oldtime New England families and their individual descendants to perfection. Then she said, 'Tell me your reconstruction of my husband's character, Sergeant.'

Lorillard's appraisal of Carlysle Stevens's *character* was essentially as his wife had just hinted; it was his appraisal of the dead man's *personality* that was different. He explained the difference first, then he said, 'Your husband kept Joshua Brewster from going through bankruptcy one time. But you'd know about that, Katie. And your husband saw Henry Winslow through a critical emotional and financial time when his mother died. Then there was the matter of George Macklin's dying wife, and your husband moved in to help in that instance too.'

Katie said, 'Sergeant, he had a public argument with George later, and he growled at Henry Winslow too.'

'Of course. And in case you didn't know it, Katie, he used to go by the hardware store and glare at Brewster until the loan was repaid. But you realise those things had to be done; that was all part of the acceptable New England personality, lest otherwise someone might accuse your husband of doing those things out of pity and sympathy.'

'You've done a very good job of reconstructing both Carlysle's motives and his feelings, Sergeant. He worked just as diligently at being considered the traditional New Englander as he ever worked at making money. Harder, I think, and of course in time he developed a genuinely flinty manner.' Katie's smile lingered. 'It was an indication of his success, of course, that everyone said he was stingy, blunt, rude and abstemious, which as you know are all compliments here in New England.'

Lorillard knew, so now he got to the point of what had brought him visiting. 'Katie, we can eliminate Brewster, Winslow and Macklin, supposedly murder-suspects. Who does that leave?'

The telephone rang. Katie excused herself to go answer it. She reappeared almost instantly to say a man named Carr would like a word with Sergeant Lorillard. He let Katie guide him to the telephone, thanked her and picked up the instrument, stating his name. At once the youthful voice of Phillip Carr came crackling down the line to him.

'Sergeant, I've just had a most interesting conversation with the newspaper editor here in town. I thought you might want to hear his theory on the Stevens matter.'

Lorillard studied a pattern in the wallpaper as he quietly said, 'Mister Carr, I'll be back at my office in something like a half hour. If you'd care to drop by at that time I'd certainly have the time to listen to new theories.'

Lorillard rang off, strolled back to the parlour where Katie was waiting, having discreetly withdrawn in order not to give any appearance of eavesdropping, and sighed as he said, 'I wonder if other trades have so many enthusiastic amateurs forever gumming up the works?' He explained about the call. Katie's reaction was sombre until he mentioned Edgar Loose, then she permitted herself a little twinkling smile.

'Mister Carr must be dense, Sergeant; most other people read one or two editions of Edgar's column and gauge him instantly.'

'Carr,' stated Lorillard, with the air of a man bearing his own small Cross, 'is young and eager.' He thanked Katie for seeing him. She went out into the garden with him where birds in treetops were actively courting or quarrelling, which seemed to be about all birds ever did unless they happened to also be hunting food.

The shade was pleasant although that filmy overcast kept any soaring heat from being troublesome, there was fragrance from Katie's roses, from her petunia beds, from a thick bed of myrtle that had dozens of small purple blossoms, and there was also the scent of wet grass to make the total blending very restful. Lorillard said her large front garden with its scents, its shade and privacy, made him envious. She had an odd reply for him.

'You are not being true to the flinty New England environment, Sergeant, which holds that men can only appreciate shade, never fragrance nor beauty, but it would certainly pleasure me if you'd come often to sit out here.'

He thought on that as he drove to the police station, decided that it would also 'pleasure' him and decided with some resolution, to do just exactly that.

Later, when Phillip Carr walked in,

Lorillard was in the act of writing something on a ruled, yellow-papered tablet. He looked up with more than a mechanical smile and welcomed his visitor with a lukewarm greeting.

Carr did not notice. He took a chair, sat perched upon the very edge of it and said, 'Mister Loose is of the opinion that —'

'Stevens was shot down by a burglar,' interrupted Lorillard. 'He's told me that before.'

'No. Not a burglar, Sergeant. He said he originally thought that on the basis of what he knew, but now he is sure the murderer is someone right here in town; someone old Stevens knew very well. Perhaps someone Stevens was accustomed to visiting. He didn't mention Mrs. Stevens, but I got the feeling, while we talked, he had her in mind — or perhaps someone equally as close.'

Lorillard said, 'That's interesting,' with sarcasm in his voice. 'Did he happen to mention, during all this theorising, who might be as close to Stevens as his wife was?'

For some reason Carr blushed. 'Well, I didn't mean it exactly that way, Sergeant. I meant, someone who was a close friend of Stevens. For example, Mister Loose mentioned Edward Arnold, the old man's brother-in-law.'

'You've met and talked to Arnold, Mister Carr. What is your judgement there?'

'Well, of course, as I told Mister Loose, Arnold is a very difficult man to imagine flying into the kind of rage one would have to feel to commit murder.'

'Stevens wasn't killed by someone in a rage, Mister Carr. He was killed by someone who definitely was *not* in a rage. Someone who had planned ahead.'

Carr accepted this, and the rock-steady but mild stare that went with it, as though it were more of a rebuke than it actually was. His resolve seemed to diminsh, his enthusiasm to crumple. 'Of course you know these people better than I do, Sergeant,' he replied. 'And I know you are very capable and all that. But you see I got a telephone call from my supervisor last night, and I'm to make a report today showing some progress in the matter of clearing up the Stevens affair.'

Lorillard had an observation to offer about the un-named supervisor who would make such an arbitrary demand. 'Man proposes, Mister Carr, God disposes. In this case if you'll come round to the hotel after dinner I'll try to give you something to use in that report to show progress. But your supervisor must be a very dogmatic person to think all he has to do is demand results and they will automatically ensue.'

After Carr departed Grady came to the door of Lorillard's office to say there had been a telephone call from Boston a couple of hours earlier, while Lorillard was out, and the caller had left a number to be used in contacting him. Then Grady, having transmitted this official bit of business, grinned and asked if Lorillard had beaten up any other suspects in his murder case.

The telephone number was Harrington, the bank examiner's private extension, and Lorillard called it with keen interest, only to be told by a girl that Mister Harrington had been called away for the balance of the day and wouldn't be back until the following morning. Lorillard thanked the girl with more equanimity than he felt, got up and marched out for his mid-day meal.

Afterwards, for no particular reason except to test the theory that Macklin would show respect now, Lorillard drove out to the garage.

Macklin did, in fact, react to the visit differently. He even bought Lorillard a bottle of Coca-Cola, dried his hands upon a wiping-rag, then joined Lorillard at the little bench where Macklin had been sitting with Edward Arnold when the dispute had broken out between them. He was friendly, relaxed and hospitable, which proved that those who had predicted this reaction in him, particularly Doctor Bradford, knew their man very well.

Macklin even joked a little, something Lorillard had never before seen the man do. Altogether, it was an enlightening little visit.

It was getting along towards mid-afternoon when Lorillard left Macklin's place and returned to the office. There were several things he wanted to do, but until he'd spoken to Harrington he decided to postpone them.

He left the station early, went to the hotel to shower and change, eat an early dinner because he preferred not being caught sitting down again by Doctor Bradford, and later he went outside to the porch for his evening pipe.

By the time Carr arrived, Lorillard was reconciled to their visit, had decided just how much — or how little — to give the younger man to keep him out of trouble with his supervisor, and since this kept Lorillard on top of the situation, he could afford to be relaxed and amiable, which he was and which he'd probably have been in any case.

14

Bingo!

Lorillard was at the office the next morning anxious to complete the call to Boston, to the office of the bank examiner, when Henry Winslow knocked, then came on in looking and acting slightly diffident. It was, Lorillard recognised, the attitude of someone not at all familiar with police stations.

He delayed making the telephone call, gave Winslow a chair and offered to fetch coffee, but Henry Winslow murmured a polite refusal. He said he very seldom touched the stuff, being a tea-drinker.

Lorillard could believe Winslow was a tea-drinker. He could also believe Winslow hadn't come calling just out of curiosity. He offered tobacco and got another refusal. Then Winslow said, sounding apologetic about it, that he'd had several weeks since the murder to reflect upon things, and the idea had occurred to him that since Joshua Brewster at one time had done quite a business in guns, including handguns, it seemed to him that if Lorillard hadn't already done so, questioning Brewster might turn up someone who'd bought a pistol at that time.

'Someone who otherwise might fit whatever is known about Carlysle's killer.'

Lorillard, who knew about Brewster's dealership in weapons some years back, had also originally had some thoughts about interrogating old Brewster, but as things had progressed this had been overlooked until now it was hardly ever pertinent.

He said, rocking back in his chair to open a desk-drawer and bring forth something wrapped in rags, 'The gun is important, Mister Winslow, but the identity of the murderer is more so.' He unwrapped the object on his desk, showing two flattened steel-jacketed bullets from a Luger pistol. 'These were dug from the wall of the room where Stevens was found.'

Winslow leaned and stared. 'They don't look right,' he murmured, and Lorillard's eyes narrowed slightly.

'Why not?'

'Well, they aren't from a thirty-two calibre automatic, Sergeant.'

'Is that a fact?'

Winslow straightened back. 'Years ago I was interested in guns. I owned several Colt thirty-twos.'

'That's what brought you down here this morning?'

'Yes. I thought someone might have remembered, and might have told you.'

No one had, but even if that had occurred Lorillard couldn't have fit Henry Winslow into the image he had of the murderer any more than he could have made it fit Katie's brother. He rolled up the smashed bullets in their oily rag and dropped them back into the desk-drawer.

Winslow said, 'I haven't owned a thirty-two in five or six years, Sergeant.'

Lorillard closed the desk-drawer very gently, raised his eyes and said, 'Mister Winslow, did I tell you Stevens was killed by thirty-two calibre bullets?'

Winslow shook his head. 'Harold Bradford told me.'

Lorillard nodded gently. 'Of course. He performed the autopsy.'

Winslow nodded. He and Lorillard talked a little longer then Winslow left, and if he'd wanted to ascertain whether or not he was a suspect, it was likely that he left just as much in the dark as he'd been when he arrived. Lorillard said nothing to set his mind at rest, but on the other hand Lorillard's friendly attitude had made it seem that he didn't suspect Winslow of being the murderer either. It was, to Henry Winslow, all very unsettling.

By eleven o'clock, when he finally had an opportunity to get that call placed to Boston, Mister Harrington was out of his office once again; this time, so the girl told Lorillard, he was in a meeting and wouldn't be out until about lunch time.

Lorillard rang off, hunted for his pipe, lit it at an hour he never smoked, and sat in quiet frustration. He could sense how close he was to confirming his suspicion but the one thing he was depending upon most strongly was eluding him.

He was about to reach for the telephone something like an hour later when it rang almost under his hand. Harrington was on the other end of the line sounding a bit pressed for time as he said, 'Sergeant Lorillard? Harrington here. We got back some data yesterday afternoon, late, that might help you a bit. Do you have a pencil handy?'

Lorillard picked one up, drew the ruled yellow tablet to him and said, 'Shoot, Mister Harrington.'

'Fifty thousand dollars was deposited, in cash — highly unusual nowadays — at the Boston National Bank on the third of last month.'

'To whose credit, Mister Harrington?'

'In a moment,' answered the bank examiner briskly. 'There was another deposit, this time of twenty-thousand dollars — which would be five thousand short of the total you gave me — the same date. This was deposited at the Massachusetts Building And Loan Corporation, here in Boston. Now then,

Sergeant, our experience substantiates the conviction that people who do as this person may have done, do not always deposit the entire sum. They usually keep a little for high-living, a new car, something like that.'

Lorillard rolled his eyes ceilingward in exasperation but did not interrupt. He was a breath away from a name which he wanted very badly, and Harrington had to go ahead and make some kind of official preachment.

'Then too, Sergeant, there is always, as in the case of this person, considerable leeway — professionally speaking you understand — for making a perfectly plausible excuse. For example, additional spadework turned up the fact that otherwise, this depositor has no large accounts anywhere in the state.'

Lorillard said a bit dryly, 'I'm prepared for that, Mister Harrington. The name please?'

'Oh. Yes of course. *Doctor Harold Bradford*.'

'Bingo!'

'. . . I beg your pardon?'

'Nothing. I'm very grateful, Mister Harrington, and of course I'll see that the proper reports are sent to you in the event of prosecution.'

'I would appreciate that, Sergeant. If at any time in the future we can serve you in any way . . .'

Lorillard rang off, whirled his chair, shot up out of it and rummaged for his old pipe. He had needed confirmation and it looked now as though he would get it.

Since his trip to Fall River the previous month he'd been able to identify the murderer. That trip, to see Doctor Bradford's niece, had turned up a very interesting bit of information: Doctor Bradford had arrived for that visit with an automatic pistol in his valise fitted with a silencer. The niece had only recalled what an odd-appearing weapon the gun had been, and when Lorillard had described a silencer she'd agreed that was what had made the gun look so unusual.

She'd told Lorillard she'd only accidentally seen the gun, when she was making the bed her uncle had used during his brief visit, in the process of which she'd upset his unlocked valise and the thing had upset, spilling out, among other things, that pistol.

But before that, Lorillard had begun to form a suspicion. Most of the people who had been close enough to Stevens, or who had at least been sufficiently acquainted with him to be on a first-name basis, had some very strong reason for *not* murdering Stevens. Usually, it was some emotional reason, and during the long course of Lorillard's experience as a policeman, he'd found that emotion more strongly than logic, motivated people one way or another. In the case of Carlysle Stevens, the people he normally would have been suspicious of, had far more reason *not* to commit murder, then they had *to* commit it.

Then there was something else. Everyone else was intrigued by the local murder almost to the point of exasperation, except Harold Bradford who only came now and then to sit at the dinnertable with Lorillard to pump him about progress.

Also, from the first moment Lorillard had satisfied himself Stevens had not died in his attic workshop, he'd speculated about just how far someone even in good physical condition, could carry the dead weight of a limp corpse. His conclusions had been that Carlysle Stevens wasn't murdered very far from home. Those suspicions were further buttressed by the later discovery that although Stevens was to visit Brewster's hardware store, not far from the Stevens residence, he'd never got there. Finally, even after nightfall it would be very awkward to carry a corpse slung over one's shoulder, for any distance at all without encountering someone.

Motive? Sergeant Lorillard was less certain of his grounds in this area, but then experience had suggested to him that motives for murder were never clear to investigators until after an arrest had been made.

Of course he had seventy-five thousand reasons for accusing Harold Bradford of the murder of Carlysle Stevens and they should have been enough, but again, Lorillard's experience had taught him to be wary of snap-judgements. It had also taught him that people with assured incomes, professional people such as medical men, rarely ever murdered just for money. Not even medical men whose practices were not large nor whose incomes, as proven in Bradford's case through Lorillard's investigation, were not very large either.

But, and here Lorillard recognised the need for caution, he could not march right out and arrest Doctor Bradford. He had enough to warrant a deeper, more thorough investigation, but not enough to file for a murder complaint through the local Grand Jury.

If he *did* file a strong complaint and couldn't support it with anything more than the suspicions he now had it was almost a mortal certainty that Doctor Bradford would flee.

The thing to be done, then, was complete the gathering of evidence until he could use that warrant in his pocket to take Bradford into custody, lock him securely in jail, then give the Commonwealth Attorney enough concrete evidence to gain a conviction against Bradford for murder.

Lorillard gazed at his watch, knocked out his pipe, went after an airline timetable, then spent an hour working out a schedule that would put him down in Boston that night, and which would return him homeward the following night.

He was confident he'd only need one full day to find out about those deposits Doctor Bradford had made. What he had in mind was gathering evidence to prove Doctor Bradford couldn't have got all that money from his medical practice — which is what Bradford would most assuredly claim if he were questioned.

It was a cardinal rule of evidence-gathering for an investigator to anticipate every claim a criminal would make and be prepared, with unshakable proof, to prove which claims were lies.

There was also something else to remember; a murderer is someone attuned to the slightest variation in an investigator's attitude, behaviour, even, as in the case of a town no larger than

Exeter, his daily routine. After all, the murderer has taken the supreme gamble: His life against the law. He cannot let down for a moment. He must know just how close the investigator may be getting. In the final analysis, he has to know when to spring up and run — literally — for his life, or when to pick up the interrupted threads of existence and go on living his life as he always had, up to the moment he committed murder.

Lorillard had to keep Doctor Bradford from suspecting he was very close to personal disaster. For that reason he had to devise a plausible excuse for not being in town the next day.

And there was one other thing Lorillard had to grapple with: Finding the murder weapon. He was satisfied Doctor Bradford had taken care that this gun should never again be seen. After all, Doctor Bradford, who performed medical chores for the police, was knowledgeable enough to realise that while ballistics was a very precise science despite its relative newness, all it could do was match a bullet to a specific gun, but if all the police had was a bullet, incriminating a felon was next to impossible.

Lorillard had to get inside the brownstone residence standing next door to Katie Stevens's house. A search-warrant wouldn't be difficult to obtain, but Exeter was not a great metropolitan community; the judge doubtless associated with Doctor Bradford. There were too many chances for pitfalls.

Lorillard didn't like the idea at all, but he saw no alternative to breaking into the Bradford place to make his search illegally. Of course if he were detected there'd be a frightful scandal, more than likely resulting in Lorillard's sacking.

But he had to find that murder-weapon. He had to have some hard, *physical* evidence. He meant to get it, too, whether it involved breaking a law or not.

First thought, he had to go to Boston. On that note Lorillard left the office, drove to the small local airport, made arrangements for the Boston-flight, then drove back to the hotel to get ready.

15

Gathering Evidence

The first tantalising scrap of information Lorillard picked up in Boston was at the offices of the Massachusetts Building And Loan Corporation, where a youthful and impeccably tailored youngish man, an executive of the company named Girard, brought forth the deposit-records for the period Lorillard questioned.

Girard was not personally acquainted with Doctor Harold Bradford, but then, as he said, Massachusetts Building And Loan was a large corporation with dozens of clerks, hundreds of other employees, and thousands of depositors; the chance that one particular depositor might be known, personally, was quite remote. Particularly when as his deposit record showed, he had over the years mailed in his usual small deposits.

Girard had another reasonable answer

for Lorillard's next question. When asked if this latest deposit by Bradford, being so much greater than any previous deposit, hadn't aroused some interest, Girard simply said, 'Sergeant, every day people are selling real estate. These are for the most part people who have never handled sums larger than a few hundred dollars. But all at once they deposit ten to twenty thousand dollars. Do you see?'

Lorillard saw. He wanted to know if the initials beside the recorded instance of deposit were those of the clerk who'd taken Bradford's money. Girard said they were. He then said, in anticipation of Lorillard's next question, 'I'll send for her, Sergeant, but you'll see: It'll be a waste of time.'

Lorillard, who hadn't been exactly wooed by the junior executive, hoped mightily Girard might be wrong just this one time. Not entirely because Lorillard wanted a definite identification of Bradford, but also because he wanted to be able to shake Girard's aplomb.

It worked out very well. The young lady, dark and leggy and liquid-eyed, who came to Girard's office, said she did, as a matter of fact, remember Doctor Bradford quite well because he had been so very pleasant, and also because his deposit had been entirely in cash — twenty thousand dollars worth — which had made her nervous, the times being as they were. She described Bradford perfectly.

Afterwards, while Girard became quite busy with a bit of lint on his arm, Lorillard said, 'You're to be commended, Mister Girard, on the kind of people you employ. The young lady's memory was perfect.'

Lorillard smiled all the way over to the Boston National Bank where he was taken at once to a private, dark-pannelled office as though he were some kind of treasonous conspirator, and was introduced to a Mister Frank Johnson, representing the bank.

In this case producing the records was delayed until Mister Johnson, hawk-faced and tough-eyed, was thoroughly satisfied about Lorillard. And even then Johnson did not act delighted over the necessity for co-operation. As he said, 'Complete privacy is something we guarantee each customer, Sergeant. It's been Boston National's policy since the Civil War.'

Lorillard was duly impressed, but he was also adamant. 'I understand perfectly,' he said pleasantly, 'and I certainly respect your rights. On the other hand it will only take me fifteen minutes to get a court order, Mister Johnson. If you'd prefer this were handled in that manner I'll go uptown and . . .'

'Sergeant Lorillard, I have not refused to produce the records. I've only sought to impress you with our position.'

'I'm impressed,' said Lorillard, still affably smiling. 'I'm also after a murderer, Mister Johnson.'

Johnson telephoned someone, gave a brusque order, turned back and offered Lorillard an expensive cigar from a beautifully tooled leather case. Lorillard declined but savoured the splendid aroma when Johnson lit up.

When the records were brought Lorillard asked if the person taking

Bradford's cash deposit could also be produced. Johnson acquiesced and this time it was a man, prim and proper and grey, and like the handsome girl at the building and loan company, this clerk also had no difficulty in recollecting Doctor Bradford. In fact, he added several comments to Lorillard's description of the doctor, and, as with the girl, he recalled Bradford most vividly because his deposit had been in cash.

He said that after accepting the deposit, he'd discreetly had the serial numbers on the notes checked by the local police against serial numbers of notes sought in connection with recent thefts, and even after this produced nothing the clerk had still wondered, although he'd done nothing further. It was, he told both Johnson and Lorillard, highly unusual for people to make such large deposits using cash.

Lorillard had what he'd come to Boston to get. After leaving the bank he went back to his hotel, packed his overnighter and took a taxi directly to the airport. There was a slight delay since he wasn't scheduled to fly back to Exeter until evening, but eventually he made a connection that enabled him to arrive back home shortly before dinner.

He was at the hotel when Lieutenant Grady called, wondering where Lorillard had been all day. It was customary to offer some kind of plausible although not necessarily true explanation, but Lorillard simply said he'd had to check on some possibilities and let it go at that.

Grady seemed satisfied. He said Phillip Carr had come by earlier in the day looking for Lorillard, and Grady chuckled over the groan that came down the line to him about that. He then also reported that Katherine Stevens had called. She had left no message although she'd told Grady she'd like Lorillard to call her back.

Lorillard considered. It was evening, he was hungry and rumpled. He decided to bathe first, eat, then drive out to the Stevens' place, and for once overlooked the possibility of a delay which he might have anticipated. Which in fact he *did* anticipate when it was too late to do anything about it.

Doctor Bradford caught him at dinner. Lorillard reflected that this made the third or fourth time. He should have guessed it might happen. By now too, he thought he should have surmised the reason: Bradford was using Lorillard as his personal straw in the wind; his source for determining if any suspicion was pointing in the doctor's direction.

As they sat, Lorillard eating, Bradford sipping tea, it posed no difficulty at all for Lorillard to act his part. When Bradford asked about new developments Lorillard chewed thoughtfully before eventually looking directly into the other man's eyes and telling a deliberate lie.

'Nothing very monumental, Doctor.' He then proceeded to say exactly what he knew Bradford wished to hear. 'What I need is a witness of some kind. Someone who either saw Stevens being carried into his residence, or who saw the murderer leaving the Stevens place afterwards. It would also help enormously if someone would come forward to report seeing an automatic pistol being thrown into a river.'

Doctor Bradford was sympathetic. 'Massachusetts has its share of rivers, but none are very close to Exeter. Still, Sergeant, you ought to be able to place *someone* near the Stevens place that night. Or perhaps you could discover that Macklin or Ed Arnold, or someone else, wasn't at home the night of the tragedy, and trace back from there to determine where they were. I've read in police magazines of criminals being caught that way.'

Lorillard smiled his gentle smile. 'Police magazines report only solved cases, Doctor, and I can tell you for a fact that for each solved case there are at least two that are *never* solved.'

Bradford nodded, finished his tea, glanced at his watch as though pressed for time, then said, 'It'll go into the local history books either way, Sergeant.' Bradford was smiling. 'But then I suppose every town is entitled to one historic riddle, eh?'

Lorillard politely agreed and resumed

eating. It was gratifying that so far at least Doctor Bradford was still quite satisfied. It was less than gratifying, however, to reflect upon the unflattering aspect of this; Bradford thought Lorillard was a big, dumb cop.

When the medical man did not depart Lorillard's curiosity was aroused. He had a feeling that Bradford had something on his mind, something he meant to mention and was perhaps seeking about for the proper means for introducing it.

Eventually Bradford said, 'Does it strike you, Sergeant, that since no one saw Carlysle being taken into his house, and that no one apparently saw him leave to go uptown to Brewster's store, that poor old Carlysle just may not have left the house?'

This of course was getting back to the same hint Bradford had dropped another time; the veiled suggestion that Katherine was involved in the murder of her husband.

Lorillard used the same argument he'd used that other time. He said, 'Granting Stevens didn't weigh much and that his widow is a sturdy woman, Doctor Bradford, it seems at bit far out to me to imagine her carrying that corpse up all those stairs to the attic.'

'I think she could have done it, Sergeant. After all, she had plenty of time. She could have put him down and rested as often as she pleased.'

Lorillard nodded. 'She could have indeed. Then there is something else: A murderer does not usually do anything that is going to point back to him — or, as in this case, to her.'

'Meaning?'

'Meaning, Doctor, if Katherine had all that time to dispose of the body my guess is that she'd have loaded him into her car and would have driven a hundred miles off to leave his body.'

Bradford smiled. 'I concede defeat,' he said. 'You have every answer, Sergeant.'

'But one, Doctor.'

Bradford shrugged that off as he said, 'You'll get that one too, I'm confident of it, Sergeant. You are an old professional. It's a case of patience and perseverance. I believe at one time you told me that was what police work was all about.'

Not long after they'd changed the subject and had discussed several other non-critical issues such as the weather, the upcoming football season, Doctor Bradford took his leave.

Lorillard didn't miss him and he felt no uneasiness over their discussion. It had come to him as they'd sat talking that he'd overlooked something in Harold Bradford throughout their earlier acquaintanceship: The man had an enormous ego.

It wasn't the kind that would make Bradford look down upon other people, specially. It was of a more subtle and rewarding variety. Bradford, an intelligent, highly-trained individual, was egocentrically brilliant, which was to say each time he spoke with someone he satisfied himself through matching wits that he was superior.

Lorillard had known a few people like that before, but not very many because in order to qualify as egocentric a person had to actually be quite intelligent, and regardless of the enormous self-esteem and righteousness education instilled in the majority of people, making them absolutely convinced they were intelligent, the bald truth was that education could not provide what heritage had already denied, therefore genuinely intelligent people, like egocentric people, were extremely rare.

Bradford, thought Lorillard as he arose to go out upon the front porch for his evening smoke, was probably going to prove to be Massachusetts' most distinguished murderer, not only in training and education but also in intelligence and oldtime Yankee heritage.

Lorillard smiled to himself. He, personally, couldn't have cared less, but he knew the majority of people would feel differently. But that didn't bother him either. He simply wanted a solid case against a murderer and he was now proceeding to build one, intelligence, heritage and training be damned.

It was a pleasant evening out, for a change. Although it had been quite warm and pleasant a week or ten days previous, up until this particular night it had been chilly again.

The imminence of summertime made some concession from Mother Nature inevitable. Perhaps this was the beginning of the change.

Lorillard sat and smoked and savoured the night, thought over once again everything he had so painstakingly created thus far, and always returned to the pair of ponderables that remained as much a riddle now as they had earlier: The whereabouts of the murder weapon, and the motive.

Bradford had with false sincerity assured Lorillard he'd solve his riddle. Lorillard now nodded, puffed on the pipe, and with the unwavering belief of a man who had been in this identical situation dozens of time before, promised himself that he'd solve the Stevens puzzle exactly as he'd solved all the other similar riddles.

16

A Visit With Katie

Lorillard drove out to the Stevens's residence after his evening smoke. He wasn't the least tired despite his rather full day. It might have been that little glow of approaching climax that kept him feeling confident and assured, but whether it was that or simply the pleasant feeling he always got when anticipating a visit with Katie, by the time he arrived, saw the orange glow of lighted windows, Lorillard was feeling both mellow and pleased.

Katie welcomed him to the parlour with a warm smile. She'd been experimenting again with her hair. This time it had been softly curved to form a dark frame for her face. It looked very attractive to Lorillard but he did not tell her so.

She asked if he'd eaten, and upon being

assured that he had and only very recently at that, she then offered to go make him a pot of coffee. He declined with a smile, saying he'd got the report of her earlier call to him through Lieutenant Grady, but that he hadn't come entirely in response to that; he'd just wanted to drop by and make sure she was all right.

She blushed, thanked him and said, 'The call wasn't important. I suppose you might call it something a woman's curiosity prompted her to do. The last time we visited I got the feeling you thought George Macklin might be involved. Or perhaps my brother.'

She was watching his face and he was aware of that. He was also aware of how diligently Doctor Bradford had sought to implicate her — not by direct accusation, never like that because it wasn't worthy of Bradford's talents — and of course if Lorillard had been willing to credit the implication he could very easily now believe she was fishing for information.

He said, 'Well, Macklin and your brother were never very prominent on my list of suspects.' Then he abruptly changed the subject. 'Was your husband a very healthy man, Katie?'

She looked blank. 'Healthy? Carlysle? I can't recall the last time he went to a doctor. I would say he was probably quite healthy for a man his age. He never complained, but then you know how that is, Sergeant. He wouldn't have complained anyway.' Katie leaned. 'Why do you ask?'

'Curious,' said Lorillard. 'Did your husband know that arthritic gentleman over on the next street named Pendelton, who owns the old Carlock place?'

Lorillard didn't care a snap whether Carlysle Stevens knew Pendelton, but he *did* care about Carlysle's relationship with Doctor Bradford, the next name he meant to introduce into their discussion. The only reason he mentioned Pendelton was to give Katie an idea he was making very general inquiries.

She sounded a little mystified when she said that as far as she knew her husband had scarcely known Pendelton. She had seen them speaking only once or twice over the back fence down the years, and she also said that, knowing her husband as she did, it seemed highly improbable he'd have much in common with Mister Pendelton.

Lorillard agreed with all this, then asked how Carlysle got along with the other neighbours, including Doctor Bradford. She thought Carlysle was civil in most cases, but, and she reiterated this, her husband had not been a man to cultivate intimacies.

'Even with Doctor Bradford, Katie?'

'That of course was something else, Sergeant. Carlysle had a small clique of friends, including Harold Bradford, Joshua Brewster and one or two others. He and Harold Bradford practically grew up together. Of course for the years that Doctor Bradford was away learning his trade they saw very little of each other.'

'But they remained friends?'

Katie nodded. 'We used to have him over for dinner quite often.'

'Used to?'

'Yes. For the past six or eight months Carlysle made no mention of it, but then he was rather busy and I didn't mention it.'

Lorillard's mild gaze drifted to Katherine and remained there. 'You didn't like Doctor Bradford?'

'Oh yes, I liked him. That is, he was always polite and well-mannered.'

'But you didn't really care for him.'

Katie turned that over in her mind before replying. 'Sergeant, Doctor Bradford is a single man. That's always a little awkward when everyone else is married. And he had an attitude . . . I can't quite describe it. It was something I could feel but could not define. At any rate, if Carlysle wanted him over for supper I was perfectly agreeable. I suppose my true feelings were simply that Harold Bradford and I, personally, had nothing in common. But I can't say I actively disliked the man.'

'Did you trust him, Katie?'

She hung fire over that answer too. 'I think he was an excellent physician, Sergeant. I had occasion to see him in his professional capacity once or twice the last few years. I always benefited from his treatments and advice.'

Lorillard nodded. She did *not* trust him, otherwise a simple 'yes' answer to his question would have been sufficient. But she could not honestly give it, so in qualifying what she said, she indicated to Lorillard, and perhaps to herself as well, that she did not trust Doctor Bradford.

'Would you like that coffee now, Sergeant?'

He smiled. 'No thank you, Katie. If you'd like we could go outside. It's a beautiful night.'

She was agreeable and led him, not out front as she'd usually done, but out into the rear garden, of which he'd only caught an occasional view on previous visits, and which he now discovered with pleasure was even more private and carefully tended than he'd thought.

There were two large old sycamore trees that shaded the north and south sides of the grounds leaving a swath of grass between. There were also several beds of roses and other cultivated perennials including a bed of delicate columbines, which were neither native to

New England nor very often found there.

Katie seemed pleased with Lorillard's expression of pleasure over the landscaping. She smiled at him, and in moonlight looked very young and sweet. 'Carlysle had his wood-working, I had my flowers,' she said. 'Some of these plants I had to send away for. That one is called a pom-pom. Local gardeners told me it wouldn't survive our winters, but as you can see it does very well. And those tea-roses — I had to put the ugly posts up to keep winter snow from breaking them.' She was animated as she explained about her plants. It was a different facet of her personality and Lorillard liked it. She was no longer the square-jawed New England housewife, unimaginative, colourless, reflecting the flintiness of her husband. She was suddenly a woman, in everything that designation implied.

Lorillard strolled over into the layers of night-time gloom beneath the northerly sycamore tree and stood quietly considering the brownstone house next door.

There were no lights, indicating that either Doctor Bradford was not at home or was abed. The house, being old and also being the product of an era of strictest functionalism, was, like the Stevens's residence, squarely set upon its ancient fieldstone foundation. It soared towards the second storey without relief of any kind, either porches or the more recent break-front porticos latter-day residents had built onto other homes like it in the community. It was actually rather grim and forbidding, even in broad daylight.

Katie came over to stand beside him and also eye the house. 'Someone from the historical society came by last year,' she said quietly, 'and took a number of photographs. It is said the Bradford place is the best example of unretouched colonial architecture in Exeter.'

He looked down, smiling. 'Early American,' he said, 'or early ugly?'

She laughed. It was a lilting, throaty sound. 'Carlysle always admired it. I'm afraid I was heretical. I always thought something should be done to it, but I never said so. You know how hidebound we New Englanders can be.'

'It's amply large for a family, Katie.'

She looked again at the house, her humour diminishing. 'Yes. But Harold never married.'

'I wonder why?'

'He was dedicated to his profession. Even as a young man I recall that he was different. Oh, he'd go on sleigh rides with the rest of us, and in summertime he'd go boating or to the music festivals. But he very rarely ever took a girl along; he'd show up as a stag. After most of our group was married, Harold seemed to fit in less and less. I suppose he just thought he was adequate unto himself, Sergeant.'

'Is he, Katie?'

She looked up again, searching his face for whatever had been behind the question. Then she dropped her eyes. 'I'm not a very worldly woman, Sergeant. I don't pretend to understand someone like Harold Bradford. I'll even go farther and admit to a feeling I didn't mention earlier when you asked whether or not I liked him. Frankly, I just don't feel at ease around him. It's as though some stone wall were between us. As I told you, he's always polite and mannerly. Professionally, he is wise and well-trained.'

'But as a man . . .?'

'I suppose that's it, Sergeant. As a man in the company of a woman — he's different.'

Lorillard pondered this briefly. He could come up with an easy and increasingly prevalent notion about all this, but somehow it just did not fit, so he fell back upon that earlier notion he'd had which branded Doctor Bradford as an egocentric.

The unique factor to this, of course, was that being a psychiatrist as well as a medical practitioner, Harold Bradford would be perhaps better qualified than nine-tenths of the people in Massachusetts to recognise the symptoms in himself. But whether he *could* or *would* diagnose himself as an egocentric Lorillard had no idea. His private notion was that Bradford's defensive mechanisms, the same as those identical reactions in other people, might very probably blind him to his personal egocentricity.

But all this was getting pretty abstract for Lorillard, the quiet, shrewd and plodding cop. Nor was he convinced it would in the final analysis be very pertinent. The law, for all its recent enlightenment, was still the law; it dealt entirely in facts and left abstractions to others.

Bradford was a murderer. Whatever else he was did not in the strictest sense, matter.

'Sergeant . . .?'

He turned and looked down into her lifted face.

'Why do you think it was Harold Bradford?'

He stood gazing at her. She was quiet and calm and obviously possessed of a good deal more depth than he'd accredited to her. He smiled. 'Are you sure that's what I think, Katie?'

'Not sure, no, but when we are together like this there seems to be some kind of — understanding — between us.'

She didn't blush when she said this, or

perhaps it was simply because they were standing in tree-shadows that he didn't think she blushed.

'My brother asked me if I thought you suspected him, Sergeant. I told him I was sure that you did not. But you've never come right out and told me you didn't. It was this feeling I get when we're together that made me tell him that.'

'And now the feeling tells you I suspect Doctor Bradford.'

She nodded without moving her eyes or speaking. Lorillard turned back to quietly study the dark house next door. 'One of the poorest things a policeman can do, Katie, before he has all the facts and all the proof, is to name names. Even to someone like you, in whom he has all the confidence in the world.'

She accepted that gentle rebuff calmly, offering only one comment. 'What possible motive would he have had, Sergeant, and if he did it, why would he have waited all these years?'

Lorillard could have answered the first part of the question easily. Seventy-five thousand dollars worth. The second part he couldn't answer, and he did not think it really applied. All that had occurred before in the lives of all these people was only pertinent in a relative way; it might, in the court hearing, point up how the crime had originally been conceived, how it had been carefully planned over the years, but none of it would very likely have much bearing on the actual murder itself.

He turned, hooked his arm through her arm and turned back towards the house. 'I'd like that cup of coffee now, Katie,' he said.

She dutifully returned to the house with him and did not mention the subject of Doctor Bradford for the balance of the evening. She was a New England woman; she held to the traditional beliefs concerning the place for a woman. It might have been an old-fashioned conviction but at least where men were concerned, it was a very pleasant and compatible one.

17

A Fresh Trail

Lorillard visited Charles Dunston at the bank the following morning with a request which Dunston honoured, but without a whole lot of enthusiasm. Lorillard wanted permission to examine the accounts, past and present, of five people whose names he'd written on a slip of paper.

Four of those people he couldn't have cared less about, the fifth one was of course, Doctor Harold Bradford. In essence what Lorillard had to discover was what connection existed between Bradford and his need for so much money. Lorillard was convinced, from the way Bradford had extorted the money, that it hadn't been a simple matter of greed or robbery.

He was also at sea about why Carlysle Stevens, after handing over the first bundle of cash, hadn't gone at once to the police, if as Lorillard was sure, he'd been a victim of extortion. And finally, Lorillard wanted to ascertain what connection existed between those two — the murderer and his victim.

He felt there had to be such a connection. He also felt it had to be very valid as far as Stevens was concerned, for otherwise Stevens would certainly have complained to high heaven about being figuratively held-up seventy-five thousand dollars worth.

Dunston was no help, but then Lorillard hardly expected him to be. Bradford had already demonstrated that he was shrewd enough not to show any increase in his local bank account after the murder, and Dunston's knowledge was pretty well limited to local matters.

It was Lorillard's hope, however, that somewhere in the past Bradford and Stevens had co-operated. He already knew, thanks to Joshua Brewster, that Carlysle Stevens was not above speculating. He knew practically nothing of Doctor Bradford's outside interests but he hoped to learn something from his current search.

Dunston offered him a tiny office, kept empty but handy for federal or state bank auditors, and from time to time Dunston peeked in at the door as Lorillard made his own kind of an audit, not very technical nor even very systematic, but thorough.

He discovered, for example, that Doctor Bradford's income was not large for a very good reason: Despite being highly skilled and certainly among the more competently trained medical men of Massachusetts, Doctor Bradford did not devote much time to his practice.

There were periods of weeks, even months, when Bradford did not see a single patient. There were also indications that Bradford had out-of-town people, probably patients, visit him at his home.

Lorillard only assumed these visitors were patients. He knew Bradford did not have many living relations and it was highly unlikely these visitors were old friends.

But the puzzling part of all this was

that, if these people were indeed patients, they seemed never to pay Bradford. At least his financial affairs reflected no compensatory infusions after the departure of these people.

Lorillard, after two hours of carefully putting together the facts about these mysterious visitations — primarily by Bradford's increased household expenses — decided he had more reason than ever to see the inside of the colonial brownstone house.

He also began to suspect that Carlysle Stevens might have somehow or other become one of those visitors, although it seemed improbable that Bradford ever encouraged other local people.

At noon Lorillard, baffled as well as hungry, closed the little office, avoided Dunston and left the bank for a brisk walk down to the hotel dining-room. He needed the stimulation of the walk to clear his mind. He also needed it to offset the hours of sitting.

But he also was brought face to face with the enigma of the visitors. He could not, for obvious reasons, corner Harold Bradford for an explanation. It was also very probable that if he asked round the neighbourhood seeking someone who might have seen people entering and leaving the brownstone residence, Bradford would hear of his enquiries and be warned.

He thought of Katie. She had lived next to Doctor Bradford all her married life. Granting that she was not a nosy or prying person, the law of averages indicated she would have noticed *something*.

Lorillard ate his lunch in haste then drove directly to the Stevens's place. Katie was baking a pie. The aroma was mouth-watering even to Lorillard who had just eaten. She had a small smudge of flour on one cheek he longed to wipe away, when she met him at the door and invited him inside.

'You're just in time,' she said, ignoring the fact that he'd been there only the previous evening and treating him as though he hadn't called round in ages. 'The pie is ready to take from the oven. It's blueberry, Sergeant, and it's piping hot.'

He almost weakened. Blueberry pie fresh from the oven was as tender as a mother's love. He smiled and shook his head. 'Katie, I need your help. I realise you don't care much for Doctor Bradford and that you're not a spying woman, but I don't know who else to go to for information about visitors Bradford has from time to time. Men and women, but that's all I know. They seem to stay from several days to several weeks. They are not local people. What I need is for you to recall seeing some of them.'

Katie's answer was calm. 'Yes, I've seen his callers. He has them frequently. Carlysle once said he thought Doctor Bradford was operating some kind of clinic next door. Carlysle also said at that time that if this were so Harold could get into difficulties with the Selectment of Exeter because our neighbourhood is not zoned for any kind of commercial enterprise.'

'Did you by any chance recognise any of them?' asked Lorillard hopefully. 'Did you hear any names or see anything that would help me locate some of those people?'

Katie shook her head. 'No. But there is someone who might be able to help. As you know, Doctor Bradford lives alone, and as you said last night, it's a rather large house. He used to employ a Mrs. O'Reilly as a maid, I believe, or as his housekeeper. She lived on the south side of town the last I heard.'

'You've seen her over there?'

'Oh yes, now and then. We never spoke although we did nod across the fence.'

'Have you seen her over there lately?'

'I think it must be two months since I last saw her. But she could have been over there. I don't usually have much occasion to be over near the north fence, Sergeant. She could even have been inside, in which case I'd not have known.'

'Do you know her first name, her address, or anything that might help me find her?'

'Yes, I may be able to help there. She is a widow, I'm quite sure of that, although I can't recall now who told me. Her son is one of Joshua Brewster's clerks at the hardware store. They call him Jack although I believe his name is Sean.'

Lorillard smiled. 'Good girl,' he said. 'Now if you'll save me a piece of the pie I'll be back this evening.'

'I'll save you the whole pie, Sergeant.'

Lorillard left in a bit of a hurry, drove to Brewster's store, and did not seek out Sean O'Reilly at all. He instead fell into a long and rambling conversation with old Brewster which included a rather general discussion of the difficulties attendant upon hiring worthwhile young clerks nowadays, and during the course of this dissertation old Brewster said, 'Except for them being local lads I'd never be able to keep O'Reilly and Johnny Cohn, my other experienced clerk. Jack O'Reilly's mother needs his support, and that keeps him in Exeter too. Otherwise, smart as he is, I'm sure the boy'd move down to Boston and get one of those high-paying jobs. He's a clever, bright and likable lad.'

'Is that a fact? Does he live close by?'

'Over on Elm Street, Sergeant. You've probably seen it — the bungalow over there with those horrid bright green window frames.'

Lorillard hadn't seen it, or, if he had in his drives around town, he'd never noticed it before. But now he did, and he also noticed something else: The sleek, late-model car parked round back when Lorillard strolled round there seeking the back door. He guessed the car was Jack O'Reilly's substitute for a wife; it was common for those virile young men who could not for one reason or another, get married, to lavish their frustrations on expensive, handsome automobiles.

He could not raise anyone although he punched the doorbell and also thumped upon the door itself with a great meaty fist. Evidently Mrs. O'Reilly was not at home. He was leaving the area when a spry little beady-eyed crone from next door came to the hedge dividing the properties and sang out after Lorillard that Mrs. O'Reilly was visiting her sister over at the nearby village of Stowe.

Lorillard asked when she'd gone and when she might be expected back. The little old woman said she'd been gone about a week, and that each year she went over there for about two weeks, which meant, if she adhered to her usual schedule, she wouldn't be home for another week.

Lorillard wasn't satisfied with that; he had no intention of waiting a week. He thanked the old woman, drove back to his office to study a road-map, which he pocketed and took along with him to his room at the hotel where he repacked his overnighter for the drive up to Stowe. The little old woman had not given Lorillard the address of Mrs. O'Reilly's sister although she had given him her name — Florance Karnac. He anticipated no difficulty locating anyone by that name and he'd deliberately elected not to ask the address for fear that might arouse some undue interest. From now on Lorillard wished above all else to prevent Harold Bradford from learning that Lorillard was particularly interested in him.

In a large metropolitan community this would have posed no problems at all. Exeter, while not exactly a village, was still not so large someone the police might be interested in wouldn't eventually be told of it by someone a detective might interrogate.

Lorillard had the entire length of the drive to Stowe to perfect some deception on this score, but aside from the obvious stumbling-block of being the only detective on the Exeter Police Force, and recognisable as such to many people, perhaps including Doctor Bradford's sometime-housekeeper Mrs. O'Reilly, there was a specific statute prohibiting policemen from eliciting information from suspects under false pretences.

On the other hand, the moment Lorillard finished with Mrs. O'Reilly the chances were excellent that she'd reach for the telephone to inform Doctor Bradford of Lorillard's interest — and his trip.

By the time Lorillard reached Stowe, which was a delightfully picturesque New England village in a lovely setting of rolling, tree-dotted countryside, he had decided to size-up Mrs. O'Reilly before revealing his identity, and depending upon whether she seemed a woman — deathly rare indeed — who could keep her lips sealed, or whether she was not such a rare jewel, he would base his actions.

As it turned out, however, by the time he reached Stowe it was supper time, so he put up at the only hotel in town, a rickety, white-painted colonial post-inn still showing loopholes for defenders' rifles and boasting hot baths, of which Lorillard had one, then he went down to the dining-room for supper, content to let the matter of Mrs. O'Reilly wait perhaps until the following morning.

Fate willed things otherwise.

Stowe's hotel had a speciality, served three times a week without fail; potroast and fresh country potatoes. Lorillard needed additional weight on his big-boned carcass like he needed a third leg. Nonetheless he ate heartily, found the beef delicious, the potatoes soft and fluffy — and murderously starchy — and in stolid contentment ambled out to the front porch as was his custom at home to smoke his pipe.

That was where Fate intervened. He was sitting back in the darkest shadows, the night was fragrantly warm, a few strollers passed hand-in-hand, mostly quite young, and except that Stowe was considerably smaller, the buildings less modern, Lorillard could have been sitting in his favourite chair back at the Exeter hotel, when a woman trooping past to enter the hotel stopped, fixed him with an intent stare, then moved over closer and after making a bold study, said, 'Sergeant Francis Lorillard as I live and breathe.'

He removed the pipe, looked up into the round face with its pug-nose and bright, pale blue eyes, and smiled. 'Good evening, madam.'

'Y'don't know me, Sergeant, but I've seen you many times over in Exeter. I'm Stella O'Reilly.'

Lorillard got smoothly to his feet, gave Mrs. O'Reilly an elegant little courtly bow and moved a chair for her to be seated close beside him.

'It's mighty good to see someone from home,' he said, without a trace of irony. 'Have you moved to Stowe then?'

Lorillard had his prey without even having to rig up a story to explain his presence in Stowe. He also had asked the first question, which meant he had the initiative. And Lorillard, the seasoned cop, would certainly keep that initiative.

18

Mrs. O'Reilly Talks

Stella O'Reilly was a somewhat shapeless, square and durable-appearing widow of fifty-five whose hands showed signs of drudgery but whose blue eyes showed the pugnacious confidence of someone whose excellent health made the idea of living off welfare very distasteful.

She was one of those aggressive, matter-of-fact people who held to the antiquated idea that hard work was good for the body, and the equally as old-fashioned notion that church-attendance was good for the soul.

She quite lacked imagination but she made up for it with a rough variety of wit which, Lorillard felt sure, would be just as rough on herself as on anyone else. In fact, by the time he'd got the conversation steered back towards Exeter from Mrs. O'Reilly's visit to her sister in Stowe, and mentioned that handsome car her son owned, she said, 'Yes, it's a fine machine, Sergeant, and it'll do the boy good; it'll not talk back and it'll give 'im no children until he's good and ready for 'em.'

Lorillard puffed his pipe and considered the technical difficulties involved in a car bearing young ready or not, decided he'd best be wary here, technology being as phenomenally progressive as it was, and returned to the subject uppermost in his mind.

'Exeter's growing,' he said. 'I should imagine your son'll have no difficulty finding a suitable wife when he's ready. There's a regular influx of people.'

Mrs. O'Reilly made a sniffing sound. 'They don't all mean to stay, Sergeant. Exeter's got no industry. That's what it takes to bring in new blood. Industry.'

'Well, we've an excellent commercial community, Mrs. O'Reilly. There's the department store, the hardware store, car agencies, hotels, even a fine and modern hospital. Then I've heard someone's starting up a clinic.'

Mrs. O'Reilly sat a moment watching

an elderly, well-dressed couple moving along out upon the starlighted side-walk before she said, 'The boy'll get married in good time, and as I've said to 'im, he'd ought to get out of Exeter and quit his worryin' about me. I was makin' my own way when he was a nipper and I'll go right on doin' it after he's gone. It's not healthy for 'im to feel tied to a mother at his age. As for the town, Sergeant, it's not a growin' one. I've lived there most of my life. I can tell you for a fact that as long as men like Dunston and Brewster and them other old fogies can rule the roost, there'll be precious little change in Exeter.'

'Doctor Bradford seems progressive,' murmured Lorillard.

Stella O'Reilly nodded. 'Progressive, yes, but he's not of the town, really.'

'Not of the town? He lives there, practices medicine there.'

'Naw, Sergeant. You don't know the man. He treats precious few local people. His practice is state-wide, even nation-wide. He soars far beyond the confines of Exeter, believe me, Sergeant. The man's a great genius, you can take the word of someone who's been workin' for him off an' on for five years and more. His views of the local people doesn't flatter 'em any.'

'I've heard him classified as a competent enough doctor,' said Lorillard, 'hardly as a genius.'

'As I say, Sergeant, you don't know the man. His local work is mostly for charity.'

Lorillard considered; the old man Bradford had been treating at the hotel could very well fit that category. And doubtless the verifiable fact that Bradford's income from Exeter, as reflected in his bank account with Dunston's establishment, was negligible, could also substantiate Mrs. O'Reilly's words. But Lorillard already knew or was willing to accept these things. It was the topic she was skirting all around that really interested Lorillard.

'I'll concede that I know little about the man, although we've had dinner together a few times and have talked,' stated Lorillard. 'But this state-wide practice of his is new to me.'

'*Nation*-wide,' averred Mrs. O'Reilly.

'They come from all over the country, and even now an' then from foreign places to be treated by Doctor Bradford.'

'Is he a specialist then?'

'I can't say, Sergeant. All I know is that they arrive, I kept the house for him, helped him put 'em up, and he treated 'em. But it wasn't my place, you know, to go round askin' a lot of questions.'

'Perhaps not but then you did the cleaning; you'd have some idea of his speciality.'

'Some,' conceded Mrs. O'Reilly, and turned silent while she thought about something. Finally she said, 'He's of the notion, y'see, that the natives bein' so hidebound and superstitious and all it'd be better if we never talked to 'em of his clinic. I've respected his wish in this matter. But o' course you're not a native, and besides that you're an enlightened person.' Mrs. O'Reilly smiled at Lorillard. 'Doctor Bradford's a real credit to the community, Sergeant. He's tremendously educated and all, y'know.' She lowered her voice and widened her eyes. 'He knows how to co-ordinate the mind and body to prevent aging. I've never had him breathe a word of how it's done directly to me, o' course, but I've heard him talk a little to the patients as come to spend a week or so with him. He's a great physician, and what's even better he's a great psychiatrist. It's the combination, mind, that gives 'im the secret o' life.'

Mrs. O'Reilly's blue eyes were bright and steady. Her expression reflected the awe she obviously felt. 'Inverse cybernetics,' she softly said. 'I've heard him say that several times. It's the secret, Sergeant. People turn their capacity for harmonic communication inward, y'see; they teach their body and minds to live in exact harmony without any disharmony, and suddenly all the wear and tear stops. They can live indefinitely without nothin' to wear 'em down and wear 'em out.'

She reached over to pat Lorillard's knee and to nod conspiratorially at him. He sat motionless considering her. There was no doubt about her sincerity. There was no doubt either, at least in Lorillard's mind, that he had the answer to what he'd wanted to learn, and perhaps best of all he'd got his answer to what he'd wanted to learn, and perhaps best of all he'd got his answer in such a manner that Mrs. O'Reilly would scarcely run to Doctor Bradford with tales of Lorillard's interest, for she had obviously confided something in Lorillard she felt should be kept secret.

About cybernetics Lorillard knew nothing. He'd of course read any number of articles giving different viewpoints on the subject because it was no longer possible to pick up a magazine or newspaper without encountering something on this latest of all human fads. But as for understanding it, he did not and would have been the first to aver that he did not.

On the other hand, without being a confirmed or habitual cynic, Lorillard had lived a fruitful life; he had seen any number of these scientific and psuedo-scientific fads come and go. He sat there thinking to himself that while the name was new and worthy of conjecture, human nature not having changed in something like ten thousand years, was likely to prove just as impervious to this latest notion as it had to all others.

He relit his pipe. Glanced sidewards at Mrs. O'Reilly, and decided he had a pretty good idea what was going on in the Bradford brownstone residence now, and almost shook his head dolorously about it, because since the beginning of time gullible people had been squandering immense fortunes seeking treatment at the hands of charlatans like Bradford who held forth promise of a living eternity.

It had never failed to amaze Lorillard. Not just that supposedly intelligent people believed in such rubbish, but that supposedly highly skilled, educated, intelligent practitioners tried to sell the idea of something that simply and practically was not at all feasible.

But Lorillard conjectured only briefly. He was, in his professional capacity, a pragmatist. Right now he needed to know more. He said, 'I've heard of Doctor Bradford's visitors. But since there was no illegality involved it didn't interest me.'

Stella O'Reilly snorted. 'Illegality? Immortality you might have said, Sergeant, and been closer to the truth o' the matter. Doctor Bradford's a fine, a wonderful and rare kind o' a man.'

'I'm sure he's a rare kind,' conceded Lorillard. 'I'd never heard what he was doing before. It sounds very exhilarating.'

'Aye. It's that and more you can bet on that, Sergeant. Those people come in lookin' worn and dispirited. When they leave they're new people. I tell you it's the greatest privilege o' me life workin' for such a man. And I'd do it for nothin' if he was to ask.'

'But he pays well, I'm sure,' murmured Lorillard.

'That he does. He's a rich man.'

'Has he told you that?'

'Told me? Not a word. But he doesn't have to tell me. I see the people come in, Sergeant, with their mink coats and their jewels, the men dressed like millionaires. I've never heard him mention fees but even if he didn't ask any, the way those people act when they leave, I know for a fact they'd endow him heavily regardless.'

Lorillard removed the pipe, knocked it out, settled back in his chair and marvelled at the two sides of Harold

Bradford. The side he presented to Lorillard, and presumably everyone else around Exeter, which showed a somewhat gruff, rather earthy country medical practitioner, eminently respected, roughly skilled, kindly, and the other side he would have to present to his sophisticated, wealthy, private clientèle. Maybe the man *was* a genius. Maybe too what he was privately selling — this 'Inverse Cybernetics' thing — was perfectly legal. Lorillard had seen a good many of those weird theories vindicated in courts of law because no one could prove they were not at least basically beneficial to their subscribers, but there was one thing Doctor Bradford was involved in which definitely was *not* legal, and that was what Lorillard was interested in.

But there was still the thorny problem of funds, only now it was no longer simply the matter of the seventy-five thousand dollars he'd extorted from Carlysle Stevens.

Of course Bradford's private patients paid him, and paid him very well. Whether Mrs. O'Reilly knew this to be a fact or not, Lorillard, with even less proof, would have staked his life on it.

What had to be unravelled next was this mystery of money. Lorillard reconciled himself to this while he sat there steering the conversation to other topics, until Mrs. O'Reilly finally said she had to leave, that she'd come by the hotel to visit an old friend who resided there, and arose to depart.

Lorillard was charming; he'd enjoyed very much sitting with her, talking with her, meeting someone from Exeter. He did not explain the coincidence that had brought him to Stowe and Mrs. O'Reilly did not think to enquire. They parted with a mutual smile and Lorillard turned to watch the sturdy little woman march on into the hotel.

He suddenly remembered that he'd promised to come by the Stevens's place this evening and have that piece of blueberry pie.

A quick glance at his watch and an equally as swift calculation of the distance separating him from Exeter, suggested that even if he suddenly sprouted wings he couldn't possibly have bridged the gulf before midnight, which would be an inexcusable time to go calling, especially on a single woman, in a New England town, so he went upstairs to his room devising methods for overcoming Katie's justifiable annoyance over having him stand her up.

He was still thinking of that a half hour later when he bedded down. The only time he turned to the other uppermost thought was when he'd decided how he could soften Katie up.

After that he turned with a mental sigh to the matter of Doctor Bradford's new wrinkle in the field of practical science-fiction: Inverse Cybernetics.

He would get inside the Bradford house. He *had* to get inside. But while that had heretofore loomed large in his speculations as some kind of *dénouement,* after his talk with Mrs. O'Reilly this seemed to suggest only a beginning.

What he *really* needed was a list of Bradford's cybernotic-patients.

He was about to drop off when a sudden very clear and concise idea burst upon him. The Internal Revenue Service would have the answer to all that money, and since all medical expenses were a legitimate tax-deduction in the United States, the IRS would also have the names of every patient Bradford had accepted funds from!

Lorillard turned up onto his side with a great groan of contentment and closed his eyes. He would get back to Exeter first thing in the morning and launch his new many-sided investigation into the affairs of the amiable murderer, Doctor Harold Bradford.

19

The Slow-Closing Vice

A wise man, having done to a woman what Sergeant Lorillard had done, undertakes his campaign of amends early. Lorillard finished a late breakfast back in Exeter after arising quite early in Stowe and driving the full distance through a delightful early, rosy dawn, after which he went to Exeter's only flower shop, wrote the little note of apology, dropped it into the box of red roses, then went on to his office. He had fired the first soft salvo of his campaign of contrition.

Later, right around noon, he sent Katie a five-pound box of chocolates with another little personal note of apology.

Otherwise, he telephoned the Internal Revenue Service down at Boston, identified himself, and tried to elicit a little information. The youthful zealot he spoke to reproved Lorillard on the grounds that the IRS kept all taxpayer-records inviolate.

Lorillard rang off, listened to Grady reading the riot act to someone out front, then put another call to the same number down in Boston. This time he got a man who sounded older. This time too, he got an unhesitating offer of complete co-operation. The IRS man would call him back as soon as he'd teletyped to Virginia for the data Lorillard wanted on Bradford's record.

Philip Carr came knocking at the door. He complained that Lorillard seemed to be avoiding him. Actually, Lorillard had been doing no such thing. It just seemed that way. But it wasn't a bad idea.

Carr also said he'd had a long and very interesting talk with Hamilton Brewster the attorney, and had learned that among other things Edward and Katherine were direct descendants of one of the most notorious men in U.S. history.

Lorillard patiently nodded. 'That's interesting indeed, although I wonder if it has a whole lot of bearing upon the murder of Carlysle Stevens?'

'But don't you see,' insisted young Carr. 'His wife and her brother, coming of such stock . . . '

'Excuse me,' muttered Lorillard. 'You didn't put any of this in your report to your home-office I hope. It would make you look downright ridiculous. No one believes in that kind of heredity I'm afraid, and with good cause. And what else did Hamilton Brewster tell you?'

'Well, that he thinks you are not going to find the Stevens murderer.'

'I'm glad of his confidence in me,' smiled Lorillard. 'Anything else?'

'Not really. We just talked. He understood my position. He started out in life the way I'm starting out now. From there he worked his way through law school — with a little help from his brother at the hardware store. At that time, he said, the hardware store's inventory was somewhat out-of-date so along with helping him through school Joshua also had to modernise. The talk was just general. He's a nice old chap once you get to know him.'

'I'm sure he is,' conceded Lorillard,

who had never bothered to cultivate old Brewster and had no intention of doing it now.

The telephone rang.

Lorillard snatched it up wondering if it could possibly be the Internal Revenue Service so soon. He was also conscious that Phillip Carr was avidly eavesdropping.

The call was from Edgar Loose the newspaper publisher. He wanted to know what progress he could report in his paper and when Lorillard said there was nothing to report just yet, Loose said, 'The people are getting tired of all the delay, Sergeant.'

Lorillard smiled indulgently as he replied. 'I'm sure you are the spokesman of the people, Mister Loose. I'm also sure you'd rather see the real culprit brought to justice than to have me simply grab hold of someone I could make a case against.'

As Lorillard rang off Carr smiled at him, giving his head a slight shake. 'That's the most egotistical and intellectually dishonest man I've ever met,

Sergeant. You told him off just right.'

Lorillard neither wished for this oblique praise nor felt as though he wanted to utilise his time, at this moment, listening to talk like that, so he arose and said, 'I am sure you'll excuse me, Mister Carr . . . ' and crossed to hold the office door open for his visitor to depart.

Carr went, without a single protest. He seemed to have picked up considerable respect for Lorillard lately. Other times he'd complained bitterly at being brushed off.

Lorillard, alone in the office again, considered his watch, put in that call for the candy to be sent to Katie with orders for the delivery lad to drop by police headquarters for the little apologetic note which was to accompany it, then he sat waiting, turning over in his mind a number of ways for him to safely burglarise Doctor Bradford's residence.

No acceptable idea came until long after the delivery boy had been and gone. Even then the usual police methods of illegal entry did not seem very clever, so Lorillard rummaged his mind for some fresh innovation in the field of imaginative housebreaking.

When the solution came, finally, later in the afternoon, it was a corollary-idea which came to mind as a result of something that dry-voiced older man from the Internal Revenue Service had to say.

'Sergeant, it's one of the blind spots of our computerised system that unless we feed data into the machines down in Virginia, they can't detect fraud.'

Lorillard began to hope a little. This one word was what he'd wished for very much, and the IRS people did not use it lightly nor loosely.

'So you see,' went on Lorillard's Boston informant, 'until you came up with the name Harold Bradford, the address and occupation, we did not have occasion to put the thing together.'

'What thing, sir?' asked Lorillard.

'Well, without a recheck and based on what the computers have dished up thus far, Sergeant, it looks like close to two million dollars. I would guess that before the overseas investigation is through, it might run half again as much.'

'Overseas?'

'Why yes, Sergeant. Doctor Bradford has a numbered deposit account in Zürich, which we will probably not be able to touch nor even to prove is his, but he also has one in Lisbon, where the U.S. Treasury Department gets a little better co-operation.'

'That's what Bradford's been doing with all this money he makes — sending it out of the country?'

'A good deal of it. There is close to a hundred thousand dollars in two institutions in Boston, and there's a small, what may well be a household account, in Exeter. But the great majority of Doctor Bradford's money goes overseas, I should imagine, in order perhaps to hide it from the U.S. Internal Revenue Service.'

'Do you anticipate sending an investigator up here?' asked Lorillard, and when the IRS man stated unequivocally that for the amount of money involved, his agency would indeed send a man up. One of their best men in fact; someone qualified as both an investigator and an auditor, Lorillard smiled.

'He should arrive tomorrow afternoon, Sergeant. I've only just put in the request before calling you. If there could be co-operation . . . ' The IRS man cleared his throat discreetly.

Lorillard promised there would be co-operation. He even volunteered to make hotel arangements and to be on hand to welcome the investigator.

Later, when he'd elicited all the additional information from the IRS man that was available and had terminated the telephone conversation, Lorillard critically considered the hands of his watch, telephoned to have perfume sent to Katie with his name on the card, then he stoked up his pipe and decided how he would break into the Bradford place.

He would simply let the IRS man invite Doctor Bradford to police headquarters — to Lorillard's private office in fact, turned over to the IRS man for the day

— and keep Bradford there answering questions while Lorillard broke into the house and went over it from cellar to attic.

Of course Bradford would be tipped off that he was no longer entirely in the clear, at least as far as the Internal Revenue Service was concerned, and that should upset him somewhat. It might even make him suspicious that perhaps the local police were also interested in him. But by now Lorillard had enough to arrest him on if he used that arrest-warrant he was carrying about with him.

He did *not* have enough to hold Bradford, of course, and if it came down to it, he didn't have enough against the doctor yet to take him to court. But he was feeling more and more confident, now that he had discovered a very powerful ally who would prosecute Bradford unmercifully if an investigation turned up fraud, and there was no denying that there was power in numbers. It also gave Lorillard considerable encouragement realising that finally, he was close enough to smile into the face of all the scoffers and doubting-Thomases.

He made a list of people to be subpoenaed beginning with Mrs. O'Reilly and going right on down the line to Doctor Bradford's niece over at Fall River. It made a rather imposing array of names at that.

He also made a list of the things he still had to do; foremost was subpoena some of the people the IRS would have on file as having supported Bradford's private clinic, and take endless depositions. He'd be busy from here on.

Then it was nearing sundown, Lieutenant Grady came by to say he'd seen Joshua Brewster and Charles Dunston talking together at the bank and had sauntered on over to be told by Brewster that young Phillip Carr, the newcomer to town who represented some insurance company or other, was beginning to sound like a policeman. What amused Grady was that Brewster had then said Carr had been seen loitering about Katie Stevens's house the night before, doubtless in serious emulation of Sherlock Holmes.

It didn't amuse Lorillard. After Grady departed Lorillard closed his desk for the day, went to the hotel for a bath and a change, then he loitered a bit downstairs in the lobby wondering whether to eat before he drove out to Katie's house, or whether to take a chance on getting more than pie out there — if indeed, he got pie after neglecting to keep their date the evening before.

In the end he decided to chance it. Katie surely should have been softened up by now. But then too, Katie was a New Englander. Lorillard would have bet his life a female from any other section of the nation would have been softened up after his presents, but he had a little twinge as he paced past the hotel dining-room door on his way out to the car. New England ladies had a very real capacity of being adamant.

He reached the car but before he could get in and escape, Henry Winslow and George Macklin, an odd pair if there ever was one, caught Lorillard at the curbing. They wanted to know, and Macklin at least was not too bashful to ask pointblank, what fresh progress had been made in the Stevens case.

Lorillard gave them his patient, kindly smile, and said nothing very startling had been unearthed in the past six or eight hours, which was true enough, but when Macklin asked if by now Lorillard didn't have at least one worthwhile suspect, Lorillard's smile got a trifle thin, he jack-knifed down into the car, then he said, 'Ask me day after tomorrow and I think I'll be able to tell you something very interesting.'

Winslow would have gracefully accepted that. Not George Macklin, who caught hold of the car-door as though by brute force to delay the departure, and leaned low to say, 'Sergeant, Ham Brewster was by my shop today to have that asthmatic car of his tuned up, and told me he'd give anyone at all a hundred to one odds that you wouldn't be able to name Stevens's murderer within six months.'

Lorillard considered, then shifted his bulk on the car seat, fished forth his wallet and pulled out two quite large notes which he pushed into Macklin's hand. 'Place the bet, George, without mentioning this is my money, and I'll split with you.'

Lorillard then spun the starter, engaged gears and with a slow wink at Macklin and Winslow, curved away from the curbing, southward bound.

Macklin stood staring at the money in his fist until Winslow softly said, 'George, you look like a mute. Put the stuff in your pocket and let's get along.'

Macklin obeyed, but as he and Winslow proceeded on their ambling course towards the centre of town his gait kept gathering speed, until Winslow protested. Then Macklin, for no apparent reason as far as startled passers-by could see, slapped his thick leg and burst into loud peals of laughter.

'He knows, Henry. By gawd Sergeant Lorillard knows who done-in Carlysle Stevens!'

'How much money did he hand you?' Winslow wanted to know.

'A hundred dollars!'

Winslow gravely inclined his head. 'Then he certainly must know. Is that what amused you?'

'Hell no,' snorted Macklin, starting away again at a great rate. 'I had a flash of the look on old Ham Brewster's kisser in a few days when he has to fork over one thousand dollars!'

20

A Moonlit Cemetery

Katie was in a fine mood by the time Lorillard got out to her house. She had, of course, divined the purpose behind his scheme of sending flowers, chocolates and perfume, and it amused her no end.

She told him she hadn't been angry the evening before because she thought she knew Lorillard well enough to be certain he wouldn't have gone off like that unless it had been something very important.

To prove her good will she had even baked a fresh blueberry pie.

Lorillard was both relieved and delighted. He was even more pleased when shrewdly-observant Katie Stevens decided from the way he ate the pie that he needed something more substantial, and made him up a plate of excellent potroast.

She was one of those gifted people who could not make a bad meal. The more Lorillard thought on this, the more he felt like wagging his head over her selection of a husband.

Not that Lorillard had anything against defunct Carlysle Stevens, personally, but Katie Arnold had been one of those rare women brimming with talents and waiting only for the proper man to come along so she could respond to everything he brought forth from her.

Instead she had to get Carlysle Stevens.

'You're thoughtful tonight, Sergeant,' she said, refilling his cup with coffee. 'Or is it simply that you are tired from a long day?'

He was a little tired, as a matter of fact, but that was not on his mind. He mentioned Stella O'Reilly, asking if Katie remembered anything derogatory about the woman. His reason for wanting to know was basic: If he worked O'Reilly into his case against Bradford, and she came apart on the witness stand under the attack of Bradford's defence counsel because of some particular aberration Lorillard had known nothing about, the Commonwealth Attorney who would prosecute, would not like it.

Katie knew nothing derogatory. She told him, as near as she could, O'Reilly's background, her personal tragedy, which entailed the passing of her husband Mike, and the ensuing struggle to raise her son Sean. Otherwise, said Katie, Stella O'Reilly was colourless enough. People liked her. They respected her independence, her stubborn perseverance at making her own way.

'Will a defence attorney be able to put her in tears, or confuse her?' asked Lorillard, finishing his coffee and feeling heavily replete.

'I think not, Sergeant,' Katie replied. 'It might work the other way around.' Katie smiled. 'Stella O'Reilly has a reputation of being able to look after herself in any kind of company.'

Lorillard nodded and felt through his pockets for the pipe and pouch hiding there. Katie turned the tables for a change and asked *him* a question.

'Sergeant, who killed my husband?'

They sat looking at one another a moment, then Lorillard concentrated his attention on packing his pipe. 'The killer of your husband,' he said slowly, 'is not someone who will go down easily, Katie. That's why I asked about Mrs. O'Reilly. He is going to have the finest attorneys money can buy, and he is going to fight hard to keep his neck, figuratively speaking, out of the noose.'

She leaned to hand him a large wooden match, her signal to him he could light his pipe in the house. 'But you won't tell me his name,' she said, straightening back to watch him light up. 'Sergeant, do you think I'm going to rush out and warn him?'

'No, Katie.'

'Or perhaps you think I'm going to shoot him for revenge.'

'Not that either, Katie. But you just might meet him and you would react quite differently to him now, wouldn't you? And that would be the same as warning him.' Lorillard arose from the kitchen table. Katie gazed up at him then also arose. She smiled apologetically.

'Excuse me, Sergeant. Come along to the parlour, it's more comfortable in there for a man to sit and smoke.'

Lorillard was dutiful. Once they were seated he said, 'You're a wonderful cook, Katie,' puffed a moment then also said, 'I'd like to repay all this kindness by taking you to dinner.' He raised his eyes to her face. He had no idea how she would react to that proposal but he thought he knew: In New England widows did not even smile again short of a year after the passing of a spouse, and it would be at least a year and a half before they dared show any serious interest in another man.

Katie astonished Lorillard. 'You have nothing to repay me for, Sergeant. Whatever I've done, it gave me pleasure or I'd not have done it. However, if you wished I'm sure we could meet down at Boston next month where I'm going to visit friends. There are any number of splendid musicals to be seen down there.'

She smiled and Lorillard smiled back.

He had not as yet taken his holiday — called 'annual-leave' — although he'd been on the verge of taking it about the time Carlysle Stevens had got himself jinxed.

He knew nothing about musicals, had not to his recollection ever attended one, but it seemed like a pleasant way of spending a week or two — with Katie on his arm of course — so he agreed to meet her down in Boston.

She then took him outside into the warm and fragrant night where crickets chirped in the warm stillness and where the usual little gusty winds of New England were stilled.

She looked very desirable this night, with her beige dress subtly hinting at a good figure and her square, handsome features calm in the moonlight. She did not seem very much like the blunt, flinty individual Lorillard had known before, and when she unconsciously looped an arm through his arm and leaned a little as she spoke, she caused a vague stirring of unfamiliar small tumults inside Lorillard.

'Life goes on, does't it, Sergeant? I

suppose that's how it should be. A man is here briefly, makes whatever kind of impression he is strong enough to make, then he departs and all that's left is the impression, and it seems to me that it too begins to change, the moment the man is no longer around.'

He hugged her hand closed between ribs and his bent elbow, and smiled down into her face. 'Lady-philosophers are new to me. As for the coming and going of a man, I'm only qualified to say that fortunately, the ones who make only bad impressions always appear to be in the minority. My *personal* feeling, after years as a policeman, is that most men fall somewhere between the good one and the bad one.'

Katie nodded. 'That would be Carlysle,' she said softly. 'And you were wise enough to see it almost at once while a good many of the people he'd lived beside all his life, had even had business dealings with, still hadn't seen it when he died. They thought he was Exeter's private Ebenezer Scrooge.'

They strolled round back where the

privacy was even greater, and for a bit Lorillard stood in tree-darkness studying the house next door. He would be inside, over there, tomorrow; what he would find was anyone's guess — maybe nothing at all, in fact.

Katie, seeing his profile in the gloom, said, 'There's a man who makes a strong impression, Sergeant: Doctor Bradford. He is the leading citizen of Exeter. His family is one of our more historic ones.'

Lorillard was not much given to sarcasm although he was quite familiar with feelings of irony: Now, he nodded his head without looking down at Katie. Bradford's impression was going to be a lasting one all right, Lorillard was confident of that. He might even linger in Exeter's history as prominent in his peculiar way as his eminently more respectable forefathers had been in their way.

Katie gave a gentle tug as though to propel Lorillard away from his preoccupied study of the darkened house next door, and as she did so she said, 'The young people like him because he's cheery and sympathetic. The older people like him because he's of their generation and somehow manages to vindicate them with their children. And of course the elderly people think he's respectful because of the way he manages to keep the Bradford burial plot out at the old-town cemetery free of weeds and properly cared for. Even his own crypt, empty though it is, he keeps properly whitewashed and presentable.'

They were two-thirds of the way across the garden when Lorillard suddenly planted both thick legs and did not budge while he put a furrowed frown and a quizzical gaze upon Katie.

'He has a crypt already prepared for himself?'

'Oh yes. But that's quite common. Surely you've seen those things throughout New England.'

Lorillard had seen them, yes, but those were waiting for very mortal people; Harold Bradford, the proselyter of some variety of earthly immortality, was hardly the kind of person Lorillard would expect to spend much time keeping his personal after-life housing presentable. It didn't ring true somehow.

Katie, studying his face, said, 'What is it?'

He forced a smile. 'Nothing, just a thought.'

Katie's New England forthrightness made her say: 'Well, Sergeant, that kind of thinking has, I'm sure, launched navies and started armies to marching.'

He laughed, squeezed her arm against his side and said, 'All right. I was wondering what Doctor Bradford's crypt looked like.'

'No need to wonder, Sergeant. You have a car parked out front. I'll get my sweater.'

They looked at one another for as long as it took Lorillard to make up his mind, nod at her, then walked briskly ahead to hold the door for her to enter the house first.

While he was standing in the warm and pleasant old parlour it came to him that taking a lovely woman, or at least one that seemed quite lovely to him, for a moonlight drive to a cemetery must be something only a policeman would even consider.

He was prepared to nullify everything when she returned with a woolly cardigan over one arm but she gave him no opportunity to say anything, at least until they were out on the porch where she turned back to make certain the door was locked, then he said, 'Katie, why don't we simply go for a nice drive in the moonlight?'

She turned, satisfied the door was locked. 'If you wish, of course. But we can make a swing past the cemetery too. No point in wasting fuel just driving when you'll simply go out there sooner or later anyway.'

Lorillard conceded, but first he did take her for a nice little cruise through the outskirts of town where a few dogs barked and some fenced fields containing cows, horses or sheep, looked like rural paintings in some metropolitan museum where city-dwellers could stand and soothe their souls — and nerves — with the sweet serenity of natural peace and calm.

They even made a big circuit around Exeter using mostly country lanes, and this was not done exclusively in order to prolong the pleasure of the drive, but also because the cemetery they sought was quite old and had been established well beyond Exeter's limits by far-sighted ancestors who thought the town might grow out and engulf their burial grounds.

It hadn't actually, although the city limits were only about a mile off at that, so the cemetery's founders were to some degree vindicated.

Like most old-time cemeteries, this one had been established on high ground. New England, like other parts of the nation, was not immune to floodings. And the trees had been pared down to a minimum in order to negate the possibility of a forest fire destroying old headboards. Of course the gloomy forests that had once surrounded Exeter were no longer standing; in fact within the memory of the oldest living native they hadn't been standing. But that had been another precaution the earlier people had taken care to eliminate, so now, when Lorillard parked in front of the iron gate and held the door for Katie to also alight, there were only perhaps two dozen trees, mostly hand-planted elms and sycamores, covering the gently lifting greensward where neat rows of graves lay.

The older headstones were ornate, even in some instances, quite excessively lavish. But at one time that had been the custom. The newer graves were flat, their stone markers lying flush in the grass to facilitate mowing and trimming.

Without any hesitation at all, Katie led Lorillard to a curbed-in plot where markers sprouted in the grass in neat rows, each with the Bradford name expertly chiselled into that most indestructible of gravestone material, New England granite.

She pointed to several domed-over massive stone crypts, all clearly sealed and occupied, save one that had Harold Bradford's name carved over it, along with his date of birth, but with no corresponding date of death.

Lorillard strode through the tree-shaded moonlight to stand and study this formidable little edifice.

21

The Gun!

The mystery of death and the traditions connected with it were more a part of rural, village, and even town, life, than city life.

It was quite common to find unoccupied but grimly waiting crypts, very often of a predeceased wife or husband who waited for his or her mate.

In Doctor Bradford's family this did not seem a prevalent idea for although a good many Bradfords lay side by side in death, as they had lived in a married state while alive, each had his and her own plot and marker.

The other crypts, oddly enough, all belonged to unmarried Bradfords, as though some family tradition decreed that the unwedded Bradfords must lie in stone beehives above the ground rather than in the earth below.

Doubtless there was an interesting allegory of some kind connected with this practice, but at this moment in the soft-diluted moonlight, Sergeant Lorillard was not whole-heartedly interested.

He paced slowly around the crypt reserved for the still-living but evidently last earthly member of this particular branch of the Bradford clan, and made a close, interested study of the crypt itself.

It was domed over with a gently curving top, obviously completed in this manner out of respect for the fierce, bleak and inundating snows of New England's winters. Its walls were massively constructed, being, Lorillard suspected, of several tiers of brick covered with a heavy coating of reinforced cement, then, for appearance sake, smoothed over with a plaster-coating. The entire structure was not more than six feet high and perhaps five feet wide. In length it was roughly ten feet long, which was what gave Lorillard his clue as to the thickness of the walls.

The slightly higher than waist-high square opening where a body was to be placed had a square, white-painted, locked door about eighteen inches in both dimensions. Lorillard rapped the door and heard the eerie echo of hollowness beyond. He also discovered in this manner that the door was of very thick steel. Evidently either Doctor Bradford, if he'd designed this structure, or someone else who was responsible, had no intention of vandals breaking in. Lorillard bent for a closer examination of the lock, of the mighty steel door itself, and of the segment of wall that held the insert-hinges. He shook his head in wonderment. Short of a quite large charge of dynamite, once that steel door was closed for eternity and coated over with more reinforced concrete, with Doctor Bradford's earthly remains inside, no one would ever be able to open the crypt again.

Katie came to stand closer to Lorillard. She had put on her sweater although it was still pleasantly warm out. When he turned, smiling, she said, 'I don't suppose even a direct hit by a bomb could shatter that crypt, could it?'

He shook his head. 'It'd have to be a

pretty big bomb, Katie.' He rummaged his trouser pockets, brought forth a clasp-knife with several somewhat unconventional inserts between the stag handles, and while she watched in astonishment, Lorillard went to work picking the lock.

She was shocked. 'What are you doing?'

He worked with an almost casual thoroughness and replied without looking around. 'Opening the door.'

'Well, I can see that, but why?'

The lock clicked open, Lorillard caught it with his free hand, studied it with professional interest and finally said, 'Curious is all.' He opened the steel door. It grated making an unpleasant sound. Inside, there was a large, very dark empty space, plastered and domed like the exterior. The air was stale and chilly. Lorillard fished out matches and lit one.

Katie gasped and Lorillard stood like stone until the burning match flickered out. They were standing there looking at just one small object in the full length of that empty vault: a blue-black automatic pistol!

Lorillard struck another match, bent for a closer look, then brought forth his handkerchief, carefully dropped it over the automatic pistol and gently picked the weapon up.

Katie came out of her surprise with a quick, strange glance at Lorillard. 'Whatever made you think it would be in there?'

Lorillard, carefully wrapping the pistol in his handkerchief, smiled. 'Just a hunch when we were in your garden tonight. While you were telling me about Bradford taking care of his crypt it occurred to me that would be an ideal place to dispose of a murder-gun.'

'Murder . . . gun?'

Lorillard turned and raised his eyes. She was standing there, utterly still, looking at him with enormous eyes.

'Murder-gun,' he reiterated.

'No . . .'

He nodded. 'Now you know.'

'But . . . Harold Bradford?' She put a hand to her throat and dropped her eyes to the white-wrapped object in

Lorillard's big paw. 'Why . . . ? I can't believe it, Sergeant. Why?'

He sighed, took her arm and turned, almost neglecting to relock the steel door. From the corner of his eye he saw the yawning black hole and turned back. Afterwards, he took her slowly back to where they'd left the car.

He said nothing. She needed a moment or two for catching her breath, for organising her thoughts. Lorillard was perfectly willing that she should have it because at last he'd had a genuine bit of luck.

There was no proof this was the murder-gun but he was confident on that score. More than ever now, he had to have Doctor Bradford immobilised for one full day. He would fly the gun to Boston if he had to, for the ballistics comparison.

He debated on whether to risk an arrest before he had written verification that this was the weapon Bradford had used to kill Carlysle Stevens, and decided not to make the arrest until he was positive.

Of course if by some bizarre occurrence this was *not* the gun . . . But who else would have had a key to the crypt? This was Lorillard's clincher. If he'd found the gun in Bradford's garden, even in his car or his house, a good attorney could always sow some reasonable doubts in a jury's mind about the gun being put in any of those places.

Lorillard stopped beside the car smiling to himself. Who but the man who owned a burial vault would have a key to it, or, for the matter of that, who would think of using such a place for concealing a weapon?

Katie put up a hand to Lorillard. 'You haven't told me.'

He let the smile diminish. 'I don't exactly have that answer, Katie, except that there was seventy-five thousand dollars involved. From experience I can tell you that thousands of people have been murdered for an awful lot less money.'

He opened the car door for her. As she got in she said, 'When will you know?'

He closed the door. 'Perhaps tomorrow afternoon.'

On the drive back through Exeter to the Stevens place he told her a little more; there could be no harm in doing that, now that she knew who his prime suspect was, but when he left her at the house she raised a grave face to him in the moonlight.

'It seems like a dream,' she murmured. He could agree with that, from her standpoint, but from his own viewpoint it seemed more like the end of a long trail.

He kissed her cheek, opened the door for her but did not enter when she turned enquiringly. He simply said he would either call or come by the next day as soon as he could, thanked her for the meal, the company, the companionship, then left to drive slowly back to the hotel. By the time he reached his room he was formulating a new plan.

He lay abed for an hour thinking about it, then closed his eyes and fell asleep.

The following morning he arose early, drove to George Macklin's place, found Macklin cooking breakfast, and after overcoming the blank look of astonishment at this unusually early call, he showed Macklin the murder-gun. As he rewrapped it he said, 'I had planned on flying down to Boston with this thing myself, today, but now I've got something else to do here. I was wondering if I could get you to take the gun to the Boston police laboratory and telephone me at my office the instant they've verified the bullets that killed Carlysle Stevens came from it?'

Macklin looked from the gun to Lorillard. 'Where did you find it, Sergeant, whose gun is it?'

Lorillard was counting out notes from his wallet and acted as though he hadn't heard. 'This should cover your air fare both ways, George, and your meals. All I ask is that you get back to me the instant the lab is finished. There may be fingerprints on the gun too, although I'm not too hopeful about that but in any case, keep it wrapped in the handkerchief.'

Macklin smiled. 'Sergeant,' he said in a sly drawl. 'I'll take the gun down there for you — providing you tell me where you got it?'

Lorillard sighed. Macklin wasn't going to believe it. 'Out of an empty grave.'

Macklin blinked, studied Lorillard's face a moment, then, when Lorillard was certain he was going to ask the next question, Macklin didn't, he simply sighed, scratched the tip of his nose and eyed the pistol. 'Okay. But you'll have to give me your word you'll tell me who used that thing on old Stevens when I return. How about it?'

Lorillard nodded. 'Agreed.'

Macklin then pointed at the boiling coffee pot. 'You care for a cup?'

Lorillard hadn't eaten but he wasn't hungry. 'No thanks. George, not a word to anyone before you leave.'

Macklin nodded. 'One other thing, does this Boston police lab know I'm coming?'

'I'll go straight back now and telephone them to be expecting you,' replied Lorillard, and made his exit from the Macklin place with that as his excuse.

He got back to the police station just as

Grady was coming on duty, threw the lieutenant a brisk wave and hastened into his office leaving Grady to stare after him. Obviously, Lorillard had been up and stirring for some little time already, and just as obviously, Grady didn't believe anyone ever did that unless they had a very good reason for it. He would have followed Lorillard into the office but the telephone rang behind him and he was called to it by the graveyard-shift officer on duty.

Lorillard made that call down to the police laboratory, then he did something he *never* did so early in the day, he fished out his pipe and fired it up. Until the Internal Revenue man arrived there was little more that he could do, and according to the last information he'd received on that arrival, the IRS investigator would not appear in Exeter until later in the day, some time in the afternoon.

He smoked and thought, and finally decided to call Boston to see if the investigator couldn't be scheduled into Exeter airport earlier.

It was a bit of luck, that call. He not only got the man to whom he'd previously spoken and who'd put in the request for the investigator, but the investigator was sitting in that same Boston office, having only a few moments earlier arrived from Washington. It was agreed that the investigator emplane at once for Exeter, and finally, putting down the telephone after having promised to be there when the airplane landed, Lorillard put aside the pipe and went out to breakfast.

It was then a little past ten o'clock.

A little past eleven he went out to the airport. It was never necessary at Exeter to know which flight someone was arriving on because Exeter was served by only one airline. The worst that could happen would be a delay.

There was, but Lorillard was neither impatient — since it didn't help — nor perturbed. When the flight was finally announced Lorillard strolled out to watch it come in. The day was turning warm, the sky was glass-clear, and when the aircraft came down at the far end of the runway Lorillard began to finally feel that he was on the home-stretch.

The IRS investigator was a calm, youngish man with an easy smile and an enquiring manner. Lorillard pumped his hand, learned his name was James Parker, and took his bags out to the police sedan for the drive back to the city and the hotel.

On the way he explained everything he knew, all that he suspected, and he also told Parker what his strategy was. Parker agreed to co-operate as best he could, within the leeway allowed him under the IRS regulations, then asked if they could stop over a moment at the hotel for a bite to eat, since on the flight up from Boston no breakfast had been served.

Lorillard was perfectly agreeable. In fact, after Parker had been settled in and fed, Lorillard personally paid for the breakfast. Then they went on down to the police station where Lorillard briefed Parker and left him, while he ambled alone up through town looking for Doctor Bradford.

22

The Victim Died Twice

Harold Bradford gave the impression of never being very busy, which he never would have been if he'd been dependent upon just the local demands, but now, with no private patients — or whatever he chose to call them — at his brownstone residence, the appearance he projected of not being very busy was a fact.

Lorillard found him at the apothecary shop having a political discussion with the proprietor, who was an old friend of Bradford's evidently, since they called one another several choice and hair-raising names without a blow being struck, and when Bradford turned towards Lorillard he was wearing an easy, raffish little smile. He winked and said, 'Sergeant, this insufferable old coot really believes Eugene McCarthy had a chance against Nixon. According to him Nixon couldn't have beaten McCarthy the way he beat Hubert Humphrey to become President.'

Lorillard smiled. 'There's a chap down at my office who wants a word with you, Doctor.'

Bradford kept his little casual smile as he studied Lorillard's face. He must have decided that the detective was too relaxed and unconcerned-appearing for this to bode any evil because he shrugged, hauled himself up off the counter, called his old friend a final pithy name and walked out of the shop.

On the drive over to the police station he asked Lorillard if someone was ill. Lorillard said it wasn't that. 'The man's from the Internal Revenue Service, Doctor.'

The change was swift and obvious. Bradford's expression turned guarded. He wanted to know more. Lorillard evaded telling him anything until, leading him into the office where Agent Parker waited, Lorillard made the introductions, then said, 'Please sit down, Doctor, and explain about the money you've been sending out of the country.'

Bradford lifted his face to Lorillard as though he'd just discovered something. He had, he'd just discovered that the big, beefy, placid-acting cop wasn't just a big beefy, placid cop. It was a blow.

Parker had some papers before himself atop Lorillard's desk and he wasted no time with preliminaries. Referring to them he said, 'Doctor Bradford, you failed to declare your full gross income for the three previous years.' Before Bradford could speak, Parker then said, 'The Swiss accounts are closed to us by international law but the Portuguese accounts are not, and we know the exact amount you have deposited in Lisbon. It is several times the amount you have declared.'

Bradford was pale but he put up a valiant struggle against the shock all this occasioned. He looked from Lorillard to Agent Parker and said, 'This is a conspiracy.'

Parker sat silent gazing directly at Bradford. His expression showed neither the contempt he may have felt, nor the curiosity that was certain to be paramount with him because he knew he was sitting across the desk from a murderer.

This silence lingered until Bradford turned on Lorillard with a cold stare. 'This is going to cost you your job, Sergeant. I'm a person of some influence in Exeter.'

Lorillard let the threat go past unnoticed. 'Perhaps,' he said quietly, 'but I doubt it, Doctor, because as of this minute you are under arrest for suspicion of murder, and the people of Exeter aren't going to be very favourably impressed on that score.'

'Murder!' exclaimed Bradford, shooting both eyes wide open. 'What the devil are you talking about, Lorillard?'

'The murder of Carlysle Stevens, Doctor.'

'You're insane, Lorillard! Prove it!'

'You extorted seventy-five thousand dollars from Stevens, Doctor, then you shot him with a little .32 automatic pistol. You had that weapon in your valise when you visited your niece at Fall River. If you're interested, that gun is now at the police laboratory in Boston being matched up with the bullets that killed Stevens. I removed it from your crypt out at the old cemetery.

'As for the seventy-five thousand dollars, Doctor, a third of it was deposited in cash with the Massachusetts Building And Loan Corporation in Boston. The other two-thirds of it was deposited with the Boston National Bank.

'You made an appointment for Stevens to stop in and see you the day he was killed, after making certain he would tell his wife he had to see Joshua Brewster that same day. He never reached the hardware store. You shot and killed him in your house, when Mrs. O'Reilly had been given time off and when none of your other visitors — the ones you sold your 'inverted cybernetics' idea to — were around.'

Lorillard paused. Up to this point he was sure of everything he'd said, or else was able to deduce as much of it as he could not actually prove, but from here on he was not so sure so he proceeded carefully.

'What amazes me is that Carlysle Stevens, the hard-headed Yankee businessman, would fall for your cybernetics rubbish to the tune of seventy-five thousand dollars.'

Bradford's neck reddened but he did not interrupt. Lorillard had been watching for exactly that sign of rising temper. He pressed on.

'But of course he finally came to his senses, and you had to kill him to avoid a public disclosure of your scheme to get rich quick from those guests you kept out of sight while you were indoctrinating them — and robbing them.'

'You are a damned liar!' burst out Doctor Bradford. 'No one was robbed. Every dime I received was paid out voluntarily by my patients.'

'Combine medical hypnosis and psychiatric hypnosis, Doctor,' retorted Lorillard, 'and you've got perhaps one of the most powerful weapons ever devised for controlling the human mind. Just one question: Why didn't it work with Stevens?'

Bradford's eyes glittered as he said,

'Stevens be damned! You won't prove any of this!'

'I'll prove it,' said Lorillard still speaking quietly. 'The Internal Revenue Service has a list of those people you milked. By now I'll be able to get all the depositions I'll need. Hypnosis doesn't last forever, Doctor Bradford. Disillusion will have set in by now.'

It was noon by this time and Lorillard's stomach was complaining. He'd arisen earlier than usual this morning, and he'd eaten earlier too, so the interim between meals was greater than usual. His stomach was empty enough to be making hollow sounds.

Then the telephone rang.

Parker wordlessly handed it to Lorillard. The voice at the other end of the connection was gruff and familiar. 'Sergeant? George Macklin here. They've completed the tests.'

'And . . . ?' Lorillard scarcely breathed. His entire case rested upon the findings of the police laboratory.

'It's the gun all right, Sergeant. They're sending it back with me along with their five page report. It's the gun that was used to kill Carlysle Stevens. *With Doc Bradford's fingerprints*.'

Lorillard let out a shallow breath and took down a bigger one. 'Okay, come on home, George.' He put the telephone down carefully and looked at Doctor Bradford. 'You can refuse to talk if you like, and under the laws of Massachusetts I'm directed to tell you that anything you say from this minute on can be used in evidence against you, Doctor: You are no longer charged with *suspicion* of murder, but rather with the direct charge of murder.' He tapped the telephone lightly. 'That was the Boston Police Laboratory. They've just corroborated my evidence.' Lorillard sat back feeling enormously relieved. 'Why the devil didn't you bury that gun?'

Bradford made a little fading gesture with one hand. 'I *did* bury it.'

Lorillard and Parker exchanged a glance. Parker began gathering his papers together as he said, 'Okay, Sergeant, but if he wiggles loose we'll be waiting to pounce. Our investigation will continue;

when we're ready to file charges believe me, if he escapes you he'll still draw twenty years to life for income tax evasion.'

Parker arose, gazed dispassionately down at Bradford, seemed about to say something, then turned and winked gravely at Lorillard and walked stiffly out of the little office.

Lorillard took the chair Parker had vacated behind the desk, picked up the pipe he'd dropped in an ashtray earlier and proceeded to clean out the dottle as he said, 'Doctor, it just doesn't make sense. You didn't have to kill old Stevens. Hell, with all that wealth you've got cached away in Europe all you had to do was pack a bag and fly away.'

Bradford sighed, watched Lorillard working with the pipe, and eventually said, 'Sergeant, I don't think you can convict me. We fought. I had to shoot in self-defence.'

Lorillard wasn't surprised. He didn't believe a word of that statement but every cornered killer he'd ever encountered tried some similar, or the same, ploy. When there were no witnesses self-defence was the best excuse for cold-blooded murder a killer could come up with, and frequently juries believed it.

The difficulty here, of course, wasn't just that Carlysle Stevens had been an old man, wizened and brittle and unable to attack anyone, but that Doctor Bradford, a younger man, was larger and stronger. Then there was the reason for their dispute. Lorillard had a good idea what that was so he said, as he refilled the cold pipe, 'Doctor, why didn't you just give him back the seventy-five thousand dollars and avoid the dispute?'

Bradford looked squarely at Lorillard. The hazy, glazed sheen of pure shock was back in his eyes again. 'I tried. He wouldn't settle for that. He said he'd give the story of my private clinic to the newspapers, that he'd expose me for a quack.'

'Why would he say that?'

'Because it didn't work with him. After he'd paid me the seventy-five thousand and I undertook to transform him, he still had his physical ailments.' Bradford glanced at his hands. 'Carlysle was my one big error. I made a point of never taking people past fifty who were not in excellent health. My theory depended upon each patient being healthy.'

'Then why did you take on old Carlysle?'

Bradford looked up again. 'My usual charge was fifty thousand dollars. Carlysle offered me seventy-five thousand.'

Lorillard lit up, leaned back and smoked. 'Greed,' he murmured. 'The invariable stumbling-block. But you still didn't have to kill him. You still could have let him sing his head off while you went to Europe and lived like a king. Why, Doctor?'

'Why? Because I had a waiting list, that's why. I had no intention of sacrificing all that money just because an old fool wanted to ruin me.'

'So in the course of that last argument he attacked you.'

Bradford nodded without speaking and felt inside his coat as though for a packet of smokes, but when he withdrew his hand it was empty. Evidently he had no cigarettes with him.

Lorillard, puffing and studying the man, felt no particular animosity. Granted, Carlysle Stevens hadn't actually been the old skinflint he'd wished people to believe he was, nevertheless Stevens still did not come across as a very lovable individual, but even if he had Lorillard hadn't known the man personally so there was no private involvement one way or another.

Lorillard finally arose and gestured for Doctor Bradford to do the same. He then took his prisoner out back to the little cell-block, locked him into one of the cages and returned to the outer desk where the duty-officer was reading a book. 'Book Harold Bradford,' he said, 'for the murder of Carlysle Stevens.'

The duty-officer arose, unruffled, and picked up a pen and booking-form as he nodded. 'Okay to call the newspaper afterwards, Sergeant? The feathers'll hit the fan now, all over town.'

Lorillard agreed and strolled out to his car. It was early afternoon, Exeter was beginning to show some signs of a lazy summer; trees stood massively green and shadowy along the streets, people appeared in short sleeves, even a dog or two, ambling along, seemed touched by the heat. Lorillard knocked out his pipe, pocketed it and almost reached his car before Phillip Carr caught him.

'Sergeant — Sergeant! Macklin's disappeared!'

Lorillard gazed stoically at the younger man whose excitement made Carr's face red and sweaty, made his eyes large and dancing.

Carr, evidently mistaking Lorillard's stoic look as an expression of shocked consternation, then said, 'I tried to warn you, Sergeant. I knew all along it had to be either Macklin, Winslow or Arnold. But you wouldn't listen.'

That duty-officer appeared back at the police station doorway. 'Sergeant,' he sang out, ignoring Carr. 'Your murderer is demanding the right to telephone Ham Brewster, his attorney. How about it?'

Lorillard nodded. 'Okay, let him make

one telephone call.'

The duty-officer turned, still ignoring Carr, and reentered the building. Lorillard bent, opened the car door and climbed in. He looked up. Carr was standing there mouth agape looking from the door of the station house to Lorillard.

'Go on in,' said the detective not unkindly. 'You want to see the murderer of Carlysle Stevens, go on in and have a good look. As for George Macklin, he didn't run anywhere, I sent him on an errand.'

Lorillard punched the starter and eased his car away from the curbing leaving Carr still looking stunned.

The drive out to Katie's house wasn't very long but Lorillard was in no hurry so it seemed long. By the time he arrived out there he'd pretty well phrased the sentences he'd use to explain things to her. He'd even figured out how to make her dead husband seem less of a dupe than he'd actually been, when he'd got himself into that position where Bradford had killed him.

It wasn't a very easy thing. Lorillard would not take liberties with the truth. But he drove slowly enough, and the little distance was adequate enough, for him to be able to make Carlysle Stevens seem pretty much as he actually was, not as he wanted people to *think* he was.

Katie was out front pruning roses when Lorillard drove up. She stood in tree-shade until he strolled over, then she put aside the shears, smiled and said, 'Tea time, Sergeant. And you'll want to sit and talk, so we'll go out back. All right?'

He matched her smile with one of his own. 'All right, Katie.' He still smiled when she turned to lead the way. Something else had just occurred to him: Carlysle had one distinction, at any rate, he was a murder victim who had died twice; once over in the Bradford house, and seemingly once more in his attic workshop. Not many dead people could do that.

Other titles in the
Linford Mystery Library:

DEATH CALLED AT NIGHT

R. A. Bennett

Jimmy Ellis believes his parents have died in a car crash when as a young boy he is taken to live with relatives in Australia. The years pass happily, then the nightmare comes. Terrifying images flit through his mind in the dark — all through the eyes of a child, a witness to grisly events seventeen years before. He begins to delve into the past, and soon he finds himself on the trail of a double murderer — a murderer who is prepared to kill again.